MW01616721

Geronimo Stilton

THE GUARDIAN OF THE REALM

THE ELEVENTH ADVENTURE IN THE KINGDOM OF FANTASY

Scholastic Inc.

Published by Scholastic Inc., *Publishers since 1920*, 557 Broadway, New York, NY 10012. SCHOLASTIC and associated logos are trademarks and/or registered trademarks of Scholastic Inc.

Stilton is the name of a famous English cheese. It is a registered trademark of the Stilton Cheese Makers' Association. For more information, go to www.stiltoncheese.com.

This book is a work of fiction. Names, characters, places, and incidents are either the product of the author's imagination or are used fictitiously, and any resemblance to actual persons, living or dead, business establishments, events, or locales is entirely coincidental.

Library of Congress Cataloging-in-Publication Data available

ISBN 978-93-5275-516-5

Text by Geronimo Stilton
Original title *Il grande segreto*
Cover by Danilo Barozzi and Roberta Bianchi
Illustrations by Silvia Bigolin, Ivan Bigarella, Carla De Bernardi, Alessandro Muscillo, and Christian Aliprandi
Graphics by Daria Colombo

Special thanks to Kathryn McKeon
Translated by Julia Heim
Interior design by Kay Petronio

First edition, September 2018

Printed at EIH Ltd, Unit: Printing Press, IMT Manesar, Gurugram. Reprinted by Scholastic India Pvt. Ltd, Sept.'18, Oct.'18, Dec.'18, Jan.'19, Apr'19

A Special Story!

Hello, rodent friends! It's me, Geronimo Stilton in the fur! I bet you're wondering why I'm dressed in this funny outfit. Well, it all started not long ago when I went on my last adventure to the Kingdom of Fantasy.

On that journey I met the wise and powerful CLEVER CHAMELEON, who lives in a place called the Bright Mountains. Clever is no ordinary lizard. He's a master of martial arts and invented the Study of the Split Tongue!

Anyway, where was I? Ah yes, I was about to tell you about my latest adventure.

Hello, friends!

1

This one begins, as I said before, in a place beyond the Kingdom of Fantasy in the Bright Mountains. The Bright Mountains are outside of tiME and space . . . and to reach them you have to travel through the Kingdom of Fantasy!

Confused yet?

Well, don't pull out your WHiSKeRS, I will explain! Just get ready for another fabumouse adventure filled with dark secrets, mystical creatures, and, of course, (gulp!) danger!

THIS IS HOW IT ALL STARTED . . .

Well, I guess it would make sense if I begin at the beginning, so here goes . . . After my last trip to the Kingdom of Fantasy I had lost my title of **true knight** and I wanted to get it back. Clever Chameleon offered to be my **master** and teach me how to regain my title. He led me to his refuge on the tippy-top of the Bright Mountains.

OH, WHAT A SCARY TRIP!

CLEVER CHAMELEON

THE MASTER OF MASTERS, THE CLEVEREST LIZARD, HE WHO KNOWS THE BALANCED PATH

Born in the Thousand Year Land, Clever, also known as Clev, is a member of the Lizard Population. His skin is blue with sparkly scales, and as a chameleon he can match his color to his surroundings. He is a master of all martial arts, which he uses to defend the weak. His strength is his experience. After all, he's lived for many thousands of years!

Each one of his words is a pearl of wisdom. His advice is sought after by all those who govern in the Kingdom of Fantasy. He knows that there is always a solution, and he is an expert at finding it. His words are wise and often sharp. In other words, he's one lizard who doesn't hold back! Still, it's not his intention to get your tail in a twist. He just wants to awaken the minds of those who seek his help to better understand the meaning of life.

He prefers the title Keeper of the Peace, a duty that he has been entrusted with directly by Blossom, the Queen of the Fairies and the Kingdom of Fantasy.

They also call him the Great Master of the Balanced Path, and as such he has written one of the most important documents in the kingdom, the Scroll of the Thirty-Three Golden Rules.

SCROLL OF THE THIRTY-THREE GOLDEN RULES

Clever Chameleon, the Great Master of the Balanced Path, the Keeper of the Peace, he who teaches the youth of the Kingdom of Fantasy according to the principles of justice, truth, and balance. He believes that life must be based on love for others and respect for every form of life in nature . . . to live in harmony, with respect for one another and in universal peace.

HERE ARE THE THIRTY-THREE GOLDEN RULES OF THE CLEVER CHAMELEON:

1. Respect life in all of its forms.
2. Respect nature.
3. Respect others and their freedom.
4. Respect the ideas, habits, and customs of others.
5. Respect the laws and rules of the community.
6. Always stay calm, in every situation . . .
7. . . . and don't ever let anger get the best of you.
8. Always be kind, as kindness is a sign of strength.
9. Think of others before yourself.
10. Always be loving . . .
11. . . . and treat others as you would like to be treated.
12. Follow your dreams, if they are good and true . . .

23. Don't ever waste water, it's precious!
24. Always tell the truth; it's easier and this way you will be deemed worthy of trust.
25. Always be sincere in your actions.
26. Stay clear of gossip and never say bad things behind someone's back!
27. Always keep the secrets of those who entrust you with them.
28. Don't spy on others' conversations!
29. Be loyal and worthy of trust toward others, not just toward your friends.

13. . . . and learn to make them a reality, even if it's hard.

14. Spread love around you.

15. Always bring joy and smiles, never pain and tears!

16. Let no creature suffer because of you!

17. Don't take what is not yours.

18. Do your duty every day with joy!

19. Share what you have: food, resources, time, money!

20. Don't brag about your actions!

21. Don't harm your surroundings: plants, animals, things . . .

22. Protect and care for the water of the rivers, springs, wells, and brooks . . .

30. Always choose good, and work to let goodness triumph in the Kingdom of Fantasy or wherever you find yourself.

31. Don't judge others if you don't want to be judged.

32. Respect those weaker than you . . . .

33. . . . and help those in difficulty!

To reach the Bright Mountains we walked for **five hundred thousand** days. Well, okay, maybe it wasn't that long, but it was *exhausting*! Plus, along the way we met fantastical creatures of every kind including those . . .

 as small as the **gnomes** . . .

as large as the **giants** . . .

 as kind as the *fairies* . . .

as mythical as the
PHOENIX OF FIRE . . .

 as mysterious as the *unicorns* . . .

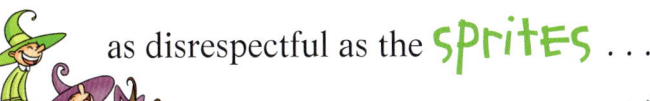

as disrespectful as the **sprites** . . .

as stinky as the **trolls** . . .

as frightening as the **ogres** . . .

as scary as the **scaly winged dragons** . . .

as terrible as the **WITCHES** . . .

GRRRR

WHAT A FRIGHT!

Even though I was exhausted, I was still **VERY** curious. So I said, "Um, Master, may I ask you a question?"

He responded with a smile and nodded.

"Well, I want to know . . . where you are taking me? Will it take much longer? What does my training consist of? Is it long? Will it be hard? Will it be scary? But most of all, why did you pick me?" I squeaked.

Clever sighed. "Ah, I will have much work to do with you! I said *one* question, but you asked me seven. I will give you just one answer," he responded.

"I don't know why I chose you, *and I am afraid that I will regret it.* But I know that soon you will have a new mission, and the safety of the entire Kingdom of Fantasy will depend on it! So, in the name of Queen Blossom, I will train you! But whether you will be able to learn *and* survive and how long it will take, this is yet to be determined . . ."

I chewed my whiskers. What did Clev mean,

IF I was able to survive? I was dying to ask more questions but I didn't. Good thing, because a minute later the chameleon insisted I not **squeak** a word until we reached some place called the **Path of the Frozen Shivers**. Brrr! Then he told me this story about the importance of **silence**.

THE CHATTY MOUSE

A young mouse went one day to a master of wisdom and began chattering up a storm. Then he said, "Oh, Master, I want to be as wise as you, and I am ready to become your student and —" The master interrupted him. "May I offer you a cup of tea?" he asked.

The mouse nodded and the master began to pour a cup of tea from a teapot. When the cup was full the master continued to pour the liquid, which spilled over.

"Master don't you see that the cup is full?" asked the mouse.

The master nodded and explained, "Just like this cup, your mind is too full of opinions and words for something else to fit inside. How can I teach you wisdom if first you don't empty your cup?"

The young mouse finally understood. In order to learn, you must first listen!

THE PATH OF THE FROZEN SHIVERS

After Clev finished speaking we took off again. Cheese niblets, my paws were **aching**! Finally, we arrived at the Path of the Frozen Shivers!

It didn't take me long to figure out how the path got its name. In front of me rose an impossibly

THE LEGENDARY PATH OF THE FROZEN SHIVERS

Clever Chameleon built this path so that his refuge would always be protected. He made sure the path was steep and very difficult to climb. It is one of the most protected places in the Kingdom of Fantasy. At the end of the path, at the top of the Bright Mountains, stands a simple wooden house, the House among the Clouds. It's equipped with everything needed to survive for a long time. Just to make sure there are no unwanted visitors, halfway down the path there is a small suspension bridge made of wood and braided rope. If he wants, the chameleon can lift it and cut off all contact with the rest of the Kingdom of Fantasy.

steep stone staircase. Just looking at it made my fur **shiver**!

After hours of climbing up the terrifyingly steep stone staircase overlooking the cliffs, we finally arrived at the top of the Bright Mountains.

There was a little house with a red roof. Tiny, colorful dragons flew in circles above it.

"Welcome to the *House among the Clouds*!" Clever announced. "This will be your home until you have finished your training. But I must warn you, whatever you do, do not bother the mini-dragons!"

Normally, the dragon warning would have made my whiskers quiver with fear, but I was so tired all I could do was collapse in a furry heap.

Flap! Flap! Flap! Flap!

BONG! BOOOONG! BOOOOOONG!

I had a terrible night, tossing and turning on top of some wicker that was placed on the floor. Aaargh, my **bones were a wreck**!

At dawn, Clever Chameleon woke me up by banging on a gigantic **GONG**.

"WAKE UP! WAAAKE UP, WAAAKE UUUP!
Student, the sun has risen! Time to get off your tail! There's no room for **laziness** along the Balanced Path!" Clever scolded.

I got up with a start and hit my head against a beam on the ceiling! **Ouch!**

"Huh? What? Who?" I **babbled**, still half asleep.

Clev huffed impatiently. He pushed me outside, then announced solemnly,

"LESSON NUMBER ONE:
He who wants to follow the Balanced Path must never laze about!

"Student, during the day you will be training constantly. To **help you** with this difficult task, I am assigning a mini-dragon to keep an eye on you. His name is **BLUEWING**. He will make sure you **keep moving** and stay busy, and most of all stop you from being a **lazy** rodent!"

BLUEWING THE MINI-DRAGON

BLUEWING is Clever's assistant and his personal dragon messenger. His secret dream is to be able to spit fire, so he eats heaps of hot peppers and constantly trains in secret . . .

THE CLAN OF THE MINI-DRAGONS

The mini-dragons are a clan of miniature dragons that come from the Colorful Desert. They were chosen by Queen Blossom to be secret winged messengers, because . . .

- They are small.

- They can blend in and hide anywhere.

- They fly in a zigzag pattern, making it hard to grab them.

- They use sonar to fly at night.

- They have a secret weapon: At the first sign of danger they can roll up and throw themselves at their enemy, hitting them with the spikes on their armor!

- They have received many medals from Blossom for their bravery.

FUN FACT:

Mini-dragons love eating spiny grub, a prickly herb that is super stinky and super spicy. Spiny grub grows only in the Colorful Desert.

I tried to protest that I was really not lazy at all. In fact, I am a very productive mouse. I mean, I am the publisher of *The Rodent's Gazette*, and I have written lots of bestselling books. My only downfall is that I am not a morning mouse.

Can I help it if I like to wake up **SLOWLY** with a hot shower and maybe a yummy cheese Danish? Hmmm . . . just thinking about food made my stomach **RUMBLE**.

But my thoughts were interrupted by a loud **SQUAWK**!

Help!

HELP!

Bluewing had **perched** on my shoulder and was *chomping* on my ear!

Then he yelled, "BLUEWING

at your service, Clever Chameleon! Don't worry. I'll get this rodent in **tip-top** shape in no time. Chest out, stand up straight, eyes on me!"

I gulped. Something told me I wasn't going to be waking up to a cheesy Danish anytime soon!

"I am leaving you in great hands, I mean **claws**," Clev chuckled, turning to me. "In nine months you will receive the Blue Belt, the first stage in your journey toward the **Balanced Path**! And now, I am off to Crystal Castle to **talk** to Queen Blossom."

Good luck!

HERE'S HOW MY TRAINING WENT . . .

THE FIRST MONTH: I LEARNED CONCENTRATION.

To train me, Bluewing forced me to shoot a bow and arrow...Too bad he kept screaming in my ear as I tried to hit the bull's-eye!

THE SECOND MONTH: I LEARNED PERSEVERANCE.

To train, I had to learn a series of super-complicated exercises . . .

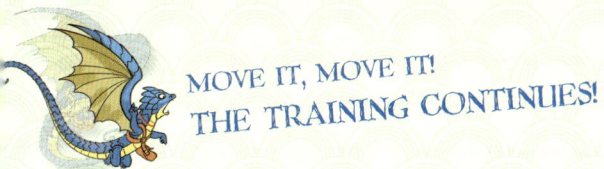

THE THIRD MONTH: I LEARNED PATIENCE.

To train, Bluewing forced me to count an enormouse pile of rice...
all the while trying to confuse me!

THE FOURTH MONTH: I LEARNED COURAGE.

To train, I was forced to sleep alone at night in the forest... as
Bluewing pretended to ambush me!

THE FIFTH MONTH: I LEARNED ORIENTATION.

To train, I had to find the road during the day by following the sun ... and then again at night by following the stars ...

THE SIXTH MONTH: I LEARNED KINDNESS.

But this was easy because I am already kind to everyone!

THE SEVENTH MONTH: I LEARNED RESPECT.

But this was also easy because I always respect everyone.

THE EIGHTH MONTH: I LEARNED THE ART OF BALANCE.

To train, I had to stay in perfect balance as Bluewing tried to make me fall by tickling me! I tried ... and tried again ... and each time I fell! But at the end of the eighth month I did it!

AND THE NINTH MONTH? I LEARNED A SECRET ART ...

The ninth month, I learned the most difficult art, the secret art of the Balanced Path ... but for now I can't tell you that one!

THE BLUE BELT OF THE BALANCED PATH

It was dawn of the very last day of the very last month of my **TRAINING** when Clever Chameleon returned.

"Master, Master, Master, Maaaaaasterrrrr!" Bluewing screamed, excitedly, jumping **UP** and **DOWN**. "Welcome back, Master! Guess what? I am totally done, done, done with the fool! I mean, well, **MORE OR LESS**, I did everything I possibly could! And it wasn't easy, let me tell you. But I did it! Basically, the student is ready to become the **THE**

GUARDIAN OF THE REALM!"

Clever Chameleon stared at me and concluded, "Student, your training is finished."

I let out a sigh of relief. "So can I go home now?" I squeaked.

Uh-oh. Within seconds the chameleon turned an annoyed shade of **red**, then **purple**, then back to **BLUE** again. "Did I say you could go home?" he snapped. "No, no. You must learn to

HAVE PITY, MASTER! I DON'T WANT TO START OVER!

Umm . . .

listen. Sheesh! If you didn't have to begin your mission so soon, I'd make you start training all over again!"

Another nine months with Bluewing screaming at me? Rat-munching rattlesnakes! This crazy adventure was turning into one big nightmare! I fell to my knees and began sobbing like a sprinkler system on HIGH SPEED.

"But, Master!" I cried. "I don't have it in me! I'm just an ordinary mouse."

For some reason this made the chameleon smile. "You are learning, student." He nodded. Then he explained that I was about to embark on an extremely DANGEROUS mission. Apparently, Queen Blossom wanted to nominate me to be her personal defender!

Instantly, I began twisting my tail in knots. Me? Why me? I mean, I don't know if I've mentioned it, but I'm a total fraidy mouse!

Clever Chameleon seemed to read my thoughts. "Don't worry," he said. "If you're ready you'll be fine, and if not . . . well, it was nice knowing you!" Then he gave me some armor and a Blue Belt.

"As for your mission, we will receive word momentarily . . ." he muttered, scanning the sky anxiously.

HOW STRANGE!

Clev explained that the special armor was known as the *Armor of Light*. The belt was the color of the sky in spring. I knelt down, and my master gave me the BLUE FABRIC belt.

I promised to honor the belt, and then I recited the *Thirty-Three Golden Rules of the Balanced Path* . . .

THE ARMOR OF LIGHT

It was forged by the most famous blacksmith in the Kingdom of Fantasy and made of blue fairy silver. It has the magical power to adapt to the body of the hero who wears it. It is warm in winter and cool in the summer and made of resistant material. It is called "the Armor of Light" because it is endowed with the power of Light, which helps whoever wears it.

THE BLUE BELT

It is a belt made of silk as blue as the morning sky. It was made by Elegantoria, a gnome tailor famouse throughout the kingdom for her ability to sew magical clothes. The Blue Belt is given to those who have passed the first stage toward the Balanced Path. It is a symbol of courage, internal strength, and kindness.

GOOD NEWS
AND BAD NEWS

It was exactly at that moment that a mini-dragon messenger FLEW toward us. His scales were dirty, and I noticed that he was wearing a silver medallion around his neck. Bluewing flew over him, worried. "Redwing, my brother, what happened? What news have you brought us?"

The **mini-dragon** huffed and puffed. "Hang on, gotta catch my breath here," the dragon coughed. Then he said, "Okay, I've got good news and I've got bad

Pant

news. Which one do you want first?"

"Good news!" I begged.

"The good news is that after nine months the queen has given birth to a beautiful baby girl. She will be the new Queen of the Realm when she grows up . . .

Princess Winglet!"

Then Redwing handed me a scroll and a **golden medallion**.

These words were written on the scroll: "**GUARDIAN OF THE REALM**, *Bright Defender, this medallion is for you. You are in charge of watching over the little princess!*"

I opened the medallion. Inside was a picture of an adorable baby. She looked exactly like Queen Blossom!

I was filled with a sense of joy. Little Winglet had the **sweetest** face.

For a minute, I forgot all about CLEVER CHAMELEON, the mini-dragons, and my training to be a true knight.

"And now for the bad news," Redwing announced, bursting my happy bubble. "Alas, little Winglet, the future of the Realm, has just been **KIDNAPPED**! The queen has called you to her palace. She needs you, Mouse, and you, too, CLEVER CHAMELEON!"

"The little princess has been kidnapped? Who would do such a horrible thing?" I squeaked.

Who could do that?

Who?
Who? Who?

"The queen is counting on you to **find out**. You must **LEAVE** at once!" Redwing insisted.

"A **DARK**, wicked, **MYSTERIOUS** shadow is headed toward the Kingdom of Fantasy," he continued.

At this Clever Chameleon began muttering under his breath, "Hmmm . . . a **DARK**, wicked, **MYSTERIOUS** shadow . . ."

Then suddenly he seemed to light up, and shouted, "Of course, why didn't I think of it before!

The Darkshadow Prophecy is coming true!"

Then he ran in the house and came back with a trunk made of pink wood, and he opened it in front of us.

It contained an ancient scroll and a spade with a crystal point, which was kept inside a blue case . . .

THE DARKSHADOW PROPHECY

C lev unrolled the scroll and read the prophecy . . .

When the Darkshadow does appear,
A treasure is stolen and replaced with fear,
Then a Bright Guardian you must find,
He who is smart and brave and kind,
With a powerful sword and a precious gem,
He must conquer the Shadow to breathe again!

Huh? I didn't understand a thing!

What was the Darkshadow? And what kind of treasure? Who was the the Guardian? I was completely confused.

Right then I noticed Clever Chameleon was **STARING** at me intensely. Then he pointed a claw at me and announced, "Student, I believe **YOU** are the **BRIGHT GUARDIAN**!"

I gulped. "M-m-me?" I stammered. "But I'm n-n-not a f-f-fighter. I mean, I'm just a m-m-mouse. Correction: I'm a 'f-f-fraidy mouse!"

The chameleon stopped me.

Whaaaat?

You are the Bright Guardian!

"We will find out soon enough. Try to draw this sword. It is called **Luminous**. It's a legendary sword, that is very **SHARP** and has great power. Only the Guardian that the prophecy speaks of will be able to draw it. No one has managed to remove it from its case for more than THOUSANDS AND THOUSANDS AND THOUSANDS OF YEARS . . ."

With my *heart* beating like a freight train, I grabbed the sword and muttered to myself, "It can't be. I'm not a Guardian. I'm a bystander . . ."

But the **SWORD** came out of its case without a struggle, with a crystal sound that **CHIMED** like a thousand **silver bells**!

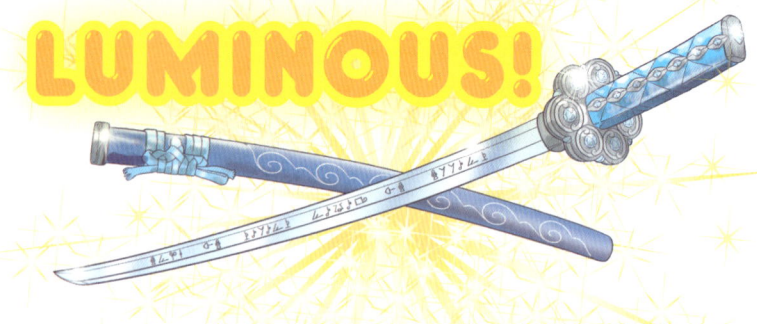

LUMINOUS!

LUMINOUS, THE SWORD OF LIGHT,
is a legendary sword that is super sharp and carries great power.
Its job is to defend the weak to insure peace in the kingdom.

MY WILL?

C lev nodded. "Well, that's it. Courageous or not, you are the **BRIGHT GUARDIAN** that the prophecy spoke of. Now quickly! We must go to the Crystal Castle!"

By now my whiskers were *twitching* with fear, but what could I do? I couldn't say no to Queen Blossom. I had to help. "Okay, I'll do it. But how will we get to the castle?" I squeaked.

"Simple!" the mini-dragon answered. "We'll go by **helidragon**. It's the fastest way to travel in the Kingdom of Fantasy! He is a dragon with golden scales that no arrow can penetrate."

A few minutes later we heard a loud flapping sound.

FLAP FLAP FLAP FLAP

In a moment, we were surrounded by a terrible **swamp smell** . . . and right then an enormouse dragon with golden scales arrived! It was the **helidragon**!

What a stench!

And in his small cabin he was carrying SCRIBBLEHOPPER, my frog friend!

Scribblehopper greeted me from afar. "Kniiiiight, I mean BRIGHT GUARDIAN, finally I found you! Quick, hop on, the queen is waiting! That's why she sent me to get you by helidragon. We're in a super rush! Though who knows if we'll get there alive. By the way, have you written your **will**?"

"My **will**? Why?" I yelled, a sense of dread running down my fur.

The frog snorted. "It's always best to take precautions before you board a helidragon. But you'll see, it will be an unforgettable experience. If you live to tell it . . ."

Clev SIGHED. "Well, it seems

SCRIBBLEHOPPER

He is a first-class literary frog. He is the exclusive advisor to Her Majesty Blossom, and Geronimo's official guide in the Kingdom of Fantasy.

we don't have any other choice. We will go by helidragon. After all, I've lived a long life . . ."

I cringed. The helidragon was sounding SCARIER than a rabid cat at a cheese festival!

Meanwhile Scribblehopper was pushing me along. "Come on, come on, stop dragging your paws," he croaked, sounding annoyed. Then he pulled a small silver box out of his pocket and threw it at me. "Here are some helipills. They may help you with air sickness. Oh, and you might as well take this paper bag, too, in case you really lose it," he added.

I was stunned. The frog, who had always been my dear friend, was being so rude. HOW strange . . .

Still, there was no time to think about it. The helidragon was waiting.

IT'S THE
DARKSHADOW!

By the time we left it was almost dawn. Before long I noticed some dark stripes on the horizon.

My heart skipped a beat. "Umm . . . that dark 'thing' . . . down there . . . what is it?" I asked nervously.

Scribblehopper rolled his eyes. "Umm . . . let's see . . . it's **sticky** . . . and gummy . . . and **stinky** . . . and **disgusting** . . . what do you think it is? It's the Darkshadow, of course!" he declared. "Sheesh! I thought you were supposed to be **BRIGHT**!"

I ignored the insult and continued, "But is it very **DANGEROUS**?"

Bluewing the mini-dragon, who was perched on my shoulder, bit my ear. "Guardiannnn! Clear

out your eardrums, that's the Darkshadow! The
D-ark-sha-dow!
D as in: **Dark**
A as in: **Amazingly wicked**
R as in: **Repulsive**
K as in: **You can't kick it!**
S as in: **Sickening**
H as in: **Horrible**
A as in: **Aaaaack!**
D as in: **Dreadful!**
O as in: **Oh, help!**
W as in: **Why me?!**"

In a flash we were immersed in a **dark cloud** that was black, as dense as tar, and was trying to surround us.

The Darkshadow

is a bewitched fog, a concentrate of the most absolute evil. It was created by Nebula, the most wicked ally of Wither, Blossom's sister. It's dense and stinky and leaves a layer that covers everything like molten lava. Wherever the Darkshadow passes, nothing ever grows again!

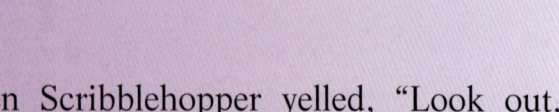

Just then Scribblehopper yelled, "Look out,
Darkshadow approaching!"

The HELIDRAGON

took off suddenly causing a
"SQUASH EFFECT"
that reached from my
stomach to my knees!

Then he darted down suddenly causing a
BOUNCE EFFECT
that jumped from my stomach
up to my tonsils!

Then he began to zigzag,

dodging clusters of dark cloud, causing a

SHAKER EFFECT

in my stomach, which sloshed

this way and that way!

WHAT AWFUL NAUSEA!

The helidragon was flying as fast as LIGHTNING . . . and I understood why Blossom had chosen it as our mode of transport!

It was only thanks to that extraordinary DRAGON that we managed to avoid those dangerous, dark CLOUD clusters that were chasing us, surrounding us, and trying to drown us like a cracker sinking into a tub of hot cheddar dip!

Finally, we left the Darkshadow behind us.

"We did it!" I celebrated.

But Clever Chameleon cut my party short. "It's true, we left it behind. But soon it will reach the CRYSTAL CASTLE and within a day it will arrive at the Fairy City!"

Rats!

SCRIBBLEHOPPER sobbed. "Ah, what a disaster! What a tragedy! What a catastrophe! Little Winglet, kidnapped . . . Crystal Castle under attack by the Darkshadow . . . the Kingdom of Fantasy in danger . . ."

He turned toward me. "But you, Bright Defender, you surely have a solution! You know, some brilliant idea! After all, you're supposed to be so IMPORTANT, so brave, so wonderful, and so smart. Well, come on, we don't have all day! What's your plan?"

Ummm . . .

Get moving!

THE FOREST KILLER!

I was more and more **STUNNED** by Scribblehopper's rudeness. Still, I **REPLIED** kindly, "I'm sorry, Scribblehopper, but for now I don't have any ideas. Mostly, because I **DON'T UNDERSTAND** what happened. How is it possible that someone managed to get into Crystal Castle and kidnap Winglet?"

How? How? How?

Clever Chameleon nodded. "Well said, student! Finally you are starting to think before you act! It seems your training wasn't useless after all!"

We traveled in the helidragon for hours . . . flying super-high above the clouds. When we approached the kingdom of fairies, I looked out, hoping to see the sparkly towers of

Here's Crystal Castle!

CRYSTAL CASTLE . . .

But instead I saw a **threatening** dark silhouette cutting across our path!

It was an enormouse flying machine shaped like a **BLACK BAT**! It had large dark wings and huge metal claws it was using to destroy the **forest**. The claws picked up trees, throwing them in a **furnace** and leaving behind a trail of **BLACK SMOKE**.

The chameleon announced solemnly, "That is Dragonster, the Forest Killer! It is Nebula's flying kingdom! Let's just hope it didn't see us or . . .

WE'RE DONE FOR!"

DRAGONSTER!
THE FOREST KILLER

It's the kingdom of Nebula, the Shadow of Desperation, the most wicked of Wither's allies. The kingdom is an enormouse, bat-shaped flying machine! It can transform from a giant bat into a mechanical dragon, a sea serpent, and more.

It can fly, swim, and fight. It's also known as the Forest Killer because it uproots trees, saws them with sharp blades, and throws the pieces into a furnace that feeds its mechanical motor.

Wherever the Dragonster goes, it leaves long, empty patches on the ground . . . where grass can never grow again!

PEE-YEW, HELISTINK!

We need to **hide** from the Dragonster! And there's only one way to do it!" Scribblehopper yelled. "We'll need to create a **helistink**. It's an enormouse stinky **CLOUD** produced by the helidragon!"

QUICKLY, Scribblehopper passed us some clothespins. "Take these and plug your noses!"

Then he turned to me. "There's only one **tiny** detail. To make this helistink, you, Bright Defender, will need to feed the helidragon tons and tons of **helibeans**."

Helibeans: The helibean plant is extremely rare and only grows in the Kingdom of the Fire Dragons. "Helibean soup" is a specialty made by crushing up the beans in large vats.

"Why me?" I protested.

"Because you're the GUARDIAN! It's your job!" Scribblehopper huffed.

His attitude was starting to really annoy me, but what could I do? I had to save us. So I began feeding the helidragon SHOVELFULS of helibeans.

Shovelful after shovelful,

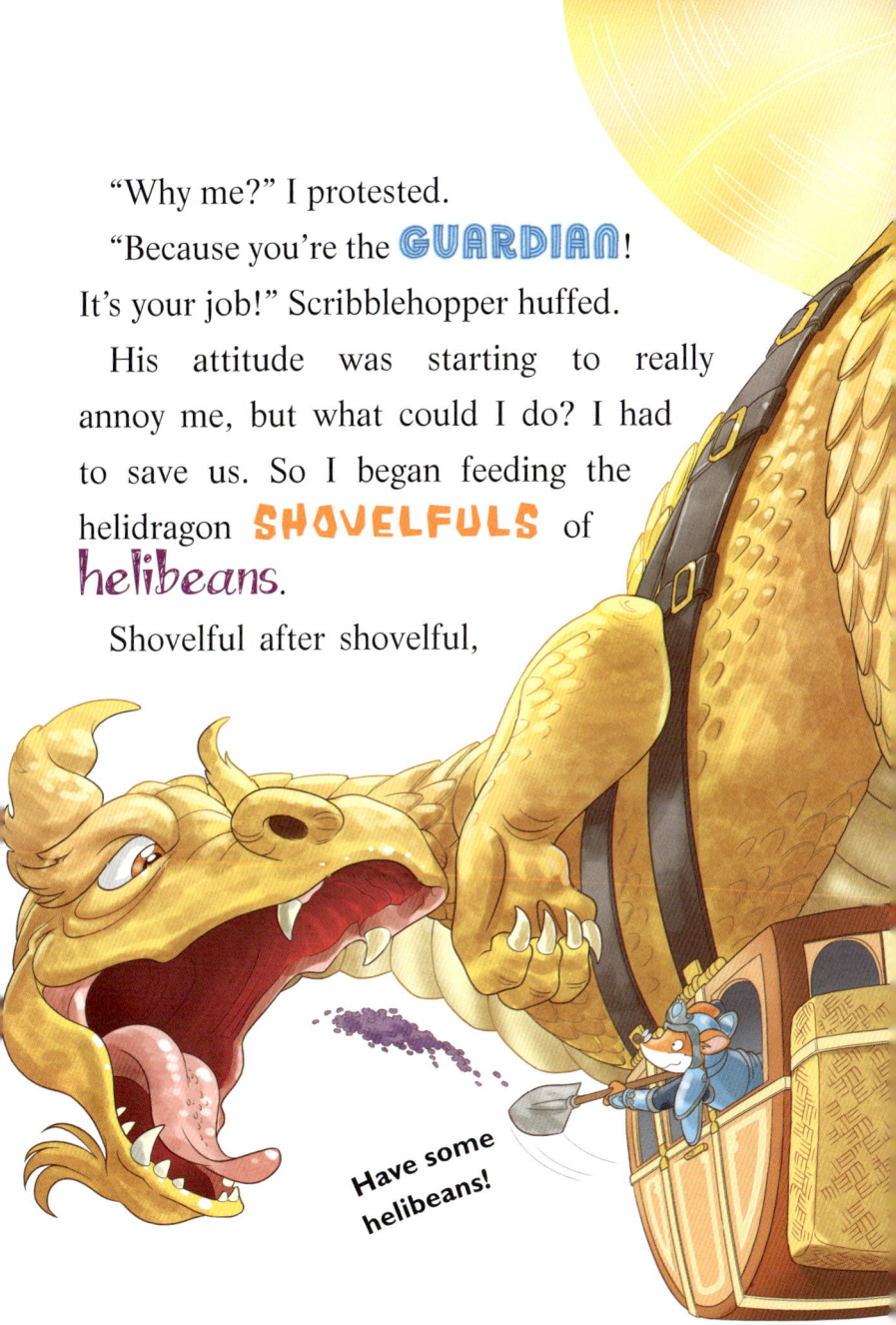

Have some helibeans!

the helidragon **devoured** all the helibeans . . . and he even licked his whiskers!

He let out a low **burp**, well actually it wasn't low. It was **super loud**! **BURP!**

"Plug up your noses!" Scribblehopper warned. "Here it comes!"

The helidragon let out a series of farts.

PUFFT! PUFFT! PUFFT! PUFFT! PUFFT! PUFFT! PUFFT!

Then he let out a really loud one.

POOOFFFFFFFFFFFFF!

That **stinky cloud** surrounded us, hiding us in the fog. **Chunky cheesy chews!** The plan worked! Now the Dragonster couldn't see us

BURP!

anymore. We were safe! But before I could celebrate, someone pushed me hard from behind. Suddenly, my squeaks of happiness turned into **shrieks** of fear as I began to fall

DOWN DOWN DOWN DOWN DOWN DOWN DOWN DOWN DOWN DOWN DOWN DOWN DOWN DOWN DOWN DOWN DOWN DOWN DOWN DOWN DOWN DOWN DOWN DOWN DOWN DOWN DOWN DOWN DOWN DOWN DOWN DOWN DOWN DOWN

As I was falling, I asked myself, *Who* **pushed** *me? And why? Or could I have fallen on my own?* **HOW STRANGE . . .**

Finally, I landed at the edge of a forest, in a green field. I was sure that I would be crushed, but luckily the **ENCHANTED ARMOR** that Clev had given me saved me!

In fact, as soon as the ground came near, the Armor of Light let out superpowerful **BLUE RAYS** of light that slowed my fall until they stopped it completely.

INCREDIBLE! IT TRULY WAS ENCHANTED ARMOR!

Help! I'll be crushed!

THWICK, THWACK!

 hankfully, I wasn't hurt. But when I stood up I saw a dark shadow on the ground. I looked up and saw . . .

THE DRAGONSTER!

The Forest Killer flew low to the ground, cutting the trees as it went with long sharp blades.

THWICK, THWACK!

Terrorized, I tried to flee, but I heard **WITHER'S** voice yelling from above, "**Stop him!** That's the Guardian of the Realm!"

Right then, a fine, **sticky net**

dropped over me. I tried to use my sword to free myself, but it didn't work. The web was a BEWITCHED SPIDER'S web!

A terrifying CHILL ran down my fur as the web lifted me up . . . higher and higher . . .

A moment later . . . I found myself inside the Dragonster, and I was all wrapped up!

A crowd of ugly wicked witches appeared, led by a CHUBBY witch I knew well. It was GROSSELDA GRIMWITCH.

I'm trapped!

To make matters worse, there was a cat there, too. It was a **BIG** black cat dressed as a wizard who was sharpening his claws and licking his whiskers! It was . . .

THE MENACE, CHATTERING CAT!

Together the crowd shouted at me,

"BUBBLE, BUBBLE, BUBBLE, YOU'RE REALLY IN TROUBLE!"

GROSSELDA GRIMWITCH!

Grimwitch is the director of the Witch School, the largest school for witches in the Kingdom. She is wicked and a traitor, and is known for being exceptionally stinky.

THE MENACE, CHATTERING CAT!

He is the assistant to Wither, Blossom's evil sister. He is disloyal, a liar, and disrespectful. He has shiny fur that's as black as ink, with one white hair on his tail. He is also the guardian of the Witch School.

THE FROG IS RIGHT HERE!

A ll the witches began to fight about what to do with me.

"Let's make a **MOUSE SOUP** with swamp rice and a side of maggots!"

"Let's have him **CLEAN** all the toilets in the Kingdom!"

"I always wanted a pet. He could be a **HOUSE**

MOUSE. I'd keep him in a cage!"

"He could be my hairmouse and shampoo my stinky hair with **slug shampoo**."

"He could wash dishes at the Wicked Witch Café."

Menace yelled, "I'm the only one who should handle him. I'm a **CAT**, so I'll just eat him! Yum!"

Eventually Grosselda got control of the crowd by shrieking at the top of her lungs, "**QUIET,**

EVERYONE, ONLY I SHALL SPEAK BECAUSE I'M IN CHARGE HERE!"

All the witches quieted down even though I heard them complaining about the **BOSSY** head witch being too big for her pointy hat.

GROSSELDA didn't seem to notice. She announced that there would be a **witch** Competition. Whoever turned me into the most original **disgusting** thing would win!

All the witches rejoiced.

"Yessss!"

"This is gonna be fun!"

POOF!   POOF!   POOF!

FROG   FLEA   LIZARD

"That rodent won't recognize his own fur when I'm done!"

Menace was the only one **grumbling** unhappily. "Humph, what a shame, wasting so much tender **MOUSE MEAT**," he sulked.

One after the other, the witches stood on a platform and yelled out ***magic spells*** . . .

Squeak, poor me!

Over and over they transformed me. First I was small. Then I was huge. Then I was hairy. Then I was covered in **feathers**.

MOSQUITO   SNAIL   SPIDER

I Won!
No, I Did!

In the end the biggest fool of them all, Witchnea, performed the final transformation. She waved her magic wand and then covered it with worm fat and yelled, *"Scurrying mouse, dumb as a flea, become a bat for all to see!"*

In a few moments I was transformed into a tiny bat with **furry** wings. It was quite disturbing being a **BAT**. I even scared myself!

At that point **GROSSELDA** shouted, "That's enough, the competition is over, we need to decide who **WON**!"

Of course, all the witches began to shriek, "I won!"

"No, I did!"

"Don't be ridiculous, I am the clear winner!"

Menace continued to meow, "Give him to me. I will turn him into **roast mouse**! Try it, you'll like it!"

Right at that moment, I realized one **positive** thing about being a bat. I had wings, which meant I could **FLY**!

Trying not to raise suspicion, I gave my new wings a tentative **flap**. They worked! I was lifting up into the air!

Then I **noticed** an open window near the ceiling. I flew like a pro to the small opening. Okay, okay, I'll be honest, I flapped along like a lame duck. Who knew **wings** were so hard to work?!

While I was flying, the witches continued arguing about who won the contest. I was thrilled. No one paid any attention to me. I flapped and I flapped.

I was definitely gaining a new APPRECIATION for flying creatures. By the time I finally reached the small window I was sweating from my little WEBBED WINGS to my little bat feet! Still, I took a deep breath and flew out into the sky. Ah, freedom!

Only then did the witches realize I was missing. "The rat is FLYING away!" I heard them shout. "You should have been watching him!" "No, it was your job!"

I wasn't surprised those witches would blame one another. Witches love to point the finger when there's a problem. What an EVIL bunch!

"I'm here!" I squeaked, spotting the helidragon in the distance.

Lucky for me, the dragon heard me and headed in my direction.

UNLUCKY for me, GROSSELDA was right on my tail, er, I mean my **wing**! She began yelling at the other witches, "Quickly, fools! Turn that bat back into a mouse!"

A moment later my bat wings disappeared and . . . *I FELL AND FELL AND*

Thank goodmouse, the helidragon was already positioned beneath me with an ENORMOUSE net. I fell straight into the net and scrambled back into the

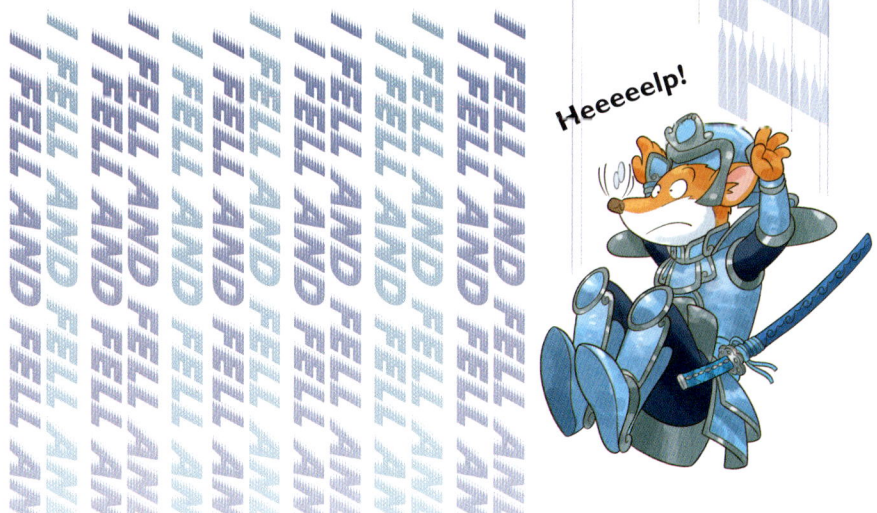

Heeeeelp!

helidragon. Whew! What a fright! I was so happy to be away from those evil witches and back with Scribblehopper and Clever Chameleon.

As the helidragon headed back toward the kingdom of fairies at full speed we cheered, "Hooray for the helidragon! Hooray for the helibeans! Hooray for the horrible stink!"

I know it may seem odd to cheer for that horrible stink. But if being stinky made the helidragon go *FASTER*, I was all for it!

Before long we could see the sparkling spires of Crystal Castle. What a mouserific sight!

The helidragon SPIRALED down toward the dragon landing pad, where the dragons who were in charge of flights were **frantically** trying to clear the area.

After a bit he slowed down his wings and, with one turn, landed gently on the pad. The mini-dragons flapped their little wings and cheered. **Flap! Flap! Flap!** What a perfect landing!

I **stumbled** off the giant gold dragon and stared up at the **shimmering** castle!

WELCOME TO CRYSTAL CASTLE

Poor Blossom!

George, Blossom's husband, greeted us along with my friend **Blue Rider** and **Solitaire**, Blossom's brother. The fairy maids of the queen were with them, along with her sister Sproutness, the seven fairy advisors, and an elderly fairy.

The fairies stood together **wringing** their

hands with concern.

"Poor Blossom!"

"It's terrible, what's happened!"

"What will we do now?"

"Kidnapped!"

George cleared a path for us. "Hurry, the queen is not doing well. The royal doctor, the gnome EmDee, is with her.

We crossed CRYSTAL CASTLE and reached the queen's quarters . . .

How awful!

We must help her!

Kidnapped!

When we reached Blossom's quarters the queen was lying on her bed. She didn't look great. I mean, usually the **Lady of Peace** has a smile on her face and a **sparkle** in her eye. Now she just stared ahead blankly.

I tried not to make a scene, but when I looked at her I started **blubbering** like a baby mouselet. Oh, how embarrassing!

How can a fairy get sick?

Fairies have very long and peaceful lives, they don't get sick, and they cannot be hurt. The only thing that can make them sick (and alas, even die) is true evil, especially if it is directed toward small and defenseless creatures . . . like Blossom's child!

When I finally got it together I managed to squeak out, "My Queen, how can I help you? I'm not the **bravest** mouse on the block but maybe there is something I could do.

Blossom tried to smile, but she couldn't. Instead she whispered, "My friend, they have kidnapped my newborn baby and now my kingdom is being threatened by the **Darkshadow**!"

Before I could respond, Clever Chameleon stepped forward. He began reading aloud the **Darkshadow Prophecy**.

When the Darkshadow does appear,
A treasure is stolen and replaced with fear.
Then a Bright Guardian you must find,
He who is smart and brave and kind,
With a powerful sword and a precious gem,
He must conquer the Shadow to breathe again!

"Never fear, *Queen Blossom*," the chameleon said. "This prophecy explains what needs to be done. You see, the most *precious* treasure that has been stolen is Princess Winglet. And the powerful sword is **Luminous**. The only one who can help destroy the Darkshadow is the **BRIGHT GUARDIAN**. He is the one who can draw the sword."

Then he passed me the **Sword of Light** and ordered, "Student, draw the sword!"

Without any trouble I drew the sword. Yep, I know it's hard to believe that I, Geronimo Stilton, was the legendary **BRIGHT GUARDIAN**! Yikes!

This is Luminous, the Sword of Light!

The fairies gasped, "**Oooooooh!**"

I took a deep breath and tried to show Blossom I was a mouse fit for the job. First I bowed before her and said, "Don't worry, My Queen, I promise on my *honor* that I will do everything in my power to find little **Winglet**. First, though, I need to figure out who stole her." I **scratched** my head and then I said, "Ahem, I will begin by examining the room where Winglet was sleeping. So, um, I need a **magnifying glass**!"

Here's the magnifying glass!

Get a magnifying glass!

Immediately, Scribblehopper **croaked** out my request.

"Get him a **magnifying glass**!" one servant told another who told another until the last servant arrived, announcing, "I've got the glass! I've got the glass!"

From the way he was carrying on you would have thought he had just won a lifetime supply of **chunky cheesy chews**!

THE ONLY THING
MISSING . . .

As soon as I got my paws on the **magnifying glass** I raced to Little Winglet's room. There, an elderly fairy stepped forward and said, "I am *Moonflower*, Princess Winglet's nurse. Let me give you a tour."

I followed the nurse around the room, which was every child's dream. There were **twinkling** lights, a **ROCKING** horse, stuffed animals, a gorgeous bassinet, books, and more. The only thing missing was the princess!

My eyes filled with tears, and for a long while I couldn't manage to look for any **CLUES**. Then I gathered my strength. *No more crying*, I told myself. I needed to find out who could be so evil as to kidnap the princess!

I started examining everything with the magnifying glass. I looked at the carpets, the curtains, the paintings, the furniture, the ornaments and decorations. There was even a statue of SCRIBBLEHOPPER. How strange . . .

Meanwhile, Scribblehopper was shouting out suggestions, yelling in my ear, "Defender, did you look behind the doors? And under the rugs? And inside the CLOSETS? Huh? Huh? Huh? Trust my frog instincts, something

Let's see here . . .

here doesn't add up!"

I tried to ask the frog to be QUiET. With all that CROAKING who could concentrate?

But he got offended and yelled in my ear once again, "I am giving you p-r-e-c-i-o-u-s advice! But if you, Defender, don't want to hear it, I will keep quiet. If things get worse, it's your own fault!"

It was then that I noticed marks on the windowsill. With the magnifying glass I took a better look. It seemed like they were left by something POINTY and sharp. Could they have been made by SHARP, POINTY . . . metal claws?!

Next I saw that there were copper **splinters** stuck

in the wood and a tear in the blue silk on the bassinet!

Could the tear have been made by something like a . . . beak?!

Last but not least, between the embroidered sheets I found a black feather!

A black . . . crow feather!

"**HOLEY CHEESE BALLS!** I figured out who it was! All the clues point to a predatory bird! It has to be

CROWBAR THE CRUEL!

"Yes, it was him, **HE** is the one that kidnapped the princess! But there is something that I don't understand. Who opened the **WINDOW** to let Crowbar in?

"Someone is a traitor, but who?"

I don't understand

CROWBAR THE CRUEL!

Crowbar, Wither's husband, is the Prince of the Darkness. He is a shape-shifting Crow, and can transform into a knight or into a crow anytime!

He is a liar like all the crows of his kind, and he loves to steal things. In the past, Wither used him to steal Blossom's enchanted Winged Ring. Geronimo was supposed to be guarding the ring, but the evil crow broke into his home and made off with it.

Crowbar lives in the Kingdom of Witches, in a nest in an enormouse dried-out baobab tree with 333 other crows that are invisible in the dark. Beware: These shape-shifting crows are extremely dangerous!

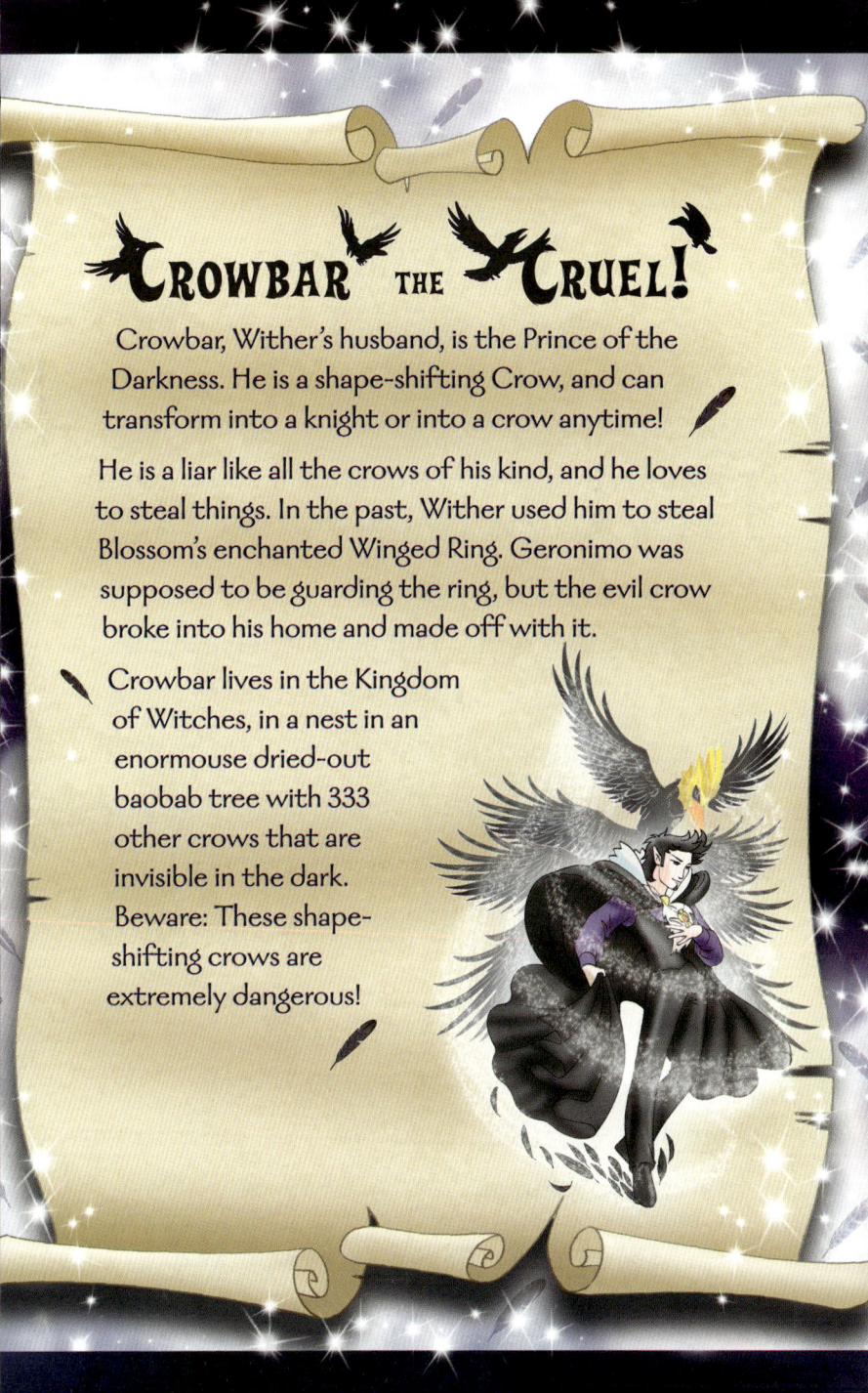

A TRAITOR AMONG US!

I returned to Blossom's quarters and shared my **terrible** discovery. "Someone has betrayed you, my queen! But who? Who would let **CROWBAR** in? Did anyone have access to **little** Winglet's room?"

Blossom gasped at the news. She explained that her trusted nurse, *Moonflower*, had access to the room. "But anyone could have entered *secretly* and opened the window," she added sadly.

The nurse burst into tears. "Oh, I will never forgive myself. I took a nap on the **ROCKING** chair and when I opened my eyes the crib was empty!" she sobbed.

"WHAT A TRAGEDY!
IT'S ALL MY FAULT!"

Blossom tried to console her. "My dear Moonflower, who could have imagined that there was a traitor among us? You gave in to sleep . . . but it could happen to anyone who has to watch over a tiny baby," she soothed.

The more Blossom spoke, the angrier she became. Just thinking of **CROWBAR** and the traitor who let him in seemed to breathe a little strength into her. With some trouble she sat up in bed and then stood up on shaky legs. "No one is to leave the castle!" she ordered. "Bright Guardian, I beg you, continue with your investigation. We

Who could have imagined?

What a tragedy!

must find the traitor and **interrogate him**! That's the first thing we need to do before we confront my wicked sister, Wither, and her husband, Crowbar!

The castle's **DOORS** were locked so that no one could **LEAVE**.

Tootutoo! Tootutoo!

Suddenly, the lookouts on the highest towers of the **castle** sounded their horns warning of danger.

Tootutoo! Tootutoo!

Then a guard ran into the room. "Your Majesty! There's an emergency! The Darkshadow is about to reach Crystal Castle!"

I ran to the window and saw a TERRIFYING SPECTACLE. The **Darkshadow** skimmed the slopes of the rock on which Crystal Castle stood.

HOLEY CHEESE BALLS, WE WERE ALL IN DANGER!

THE CRYSTAL GEM

Blossom made her way to the Ceremony Room. Luckily, she had her husband, George, to keep her upright. Twisted cattails, the queen looked **wobbly**! Still, when she sat down on her throne her voice rose confidently.

"All those who seek protection from the **Darkshadow** shall be let into these walls! We will, of course, take care of our subjects. But remember, no one may leave the castle . . . **there's a traitor among us**!" she declared.

Immediately, the doors of the castle opened and a **long** line of inhabitants of the Kingdom of Fantasy crowded around to enter . . .

As soon as the Ceremony Room was full of creatures, Blossom turned to Clever Chameleon.

"My dear friend, what do you suggest we do to stop the **Darkshadow**?"

"There is only one thing to do," the chameleon said. He pulled out the scroll with the Dark Prophecy and began reading it aloud. The words *buzzed* around in my head but at this point all I heard was . . .

BLAH, BLAH, BLAH
BRIGHT GUARDIAN
BLAH, BLAH, BLAH
POWERFUL SWORD
BLAH, BLAH, BLAH
PRECIOUS GEM
I WAS SO CONFUSED!!!!!

Don't make me look bad!

"So the GUARDIAN, which is, um . . . me, has to find a GEM, right? And where would I find it? And where do I find the Darkshadow's house or, er, cave? And um, this sounds pretty D-D-DANGEROUS. Are you sure it's a g-g-good idea?" I stammered.

At this BLUEWING the mini-dragon bit my ear. "Don't be a fool, Defender," he whispered. "Of course, it will be DANGEROUS. You will be going out on a DEADLY mission, not out for a slice of pizza!"

My stomach rumbled at the mention of pizza. Oh, what I wouldn't give to be back in New Mouse City munching on a tasty slice at the Pizza Rat!

"The precious gem is none other than the powerful CRYSTAL GEM," the chameleon explained.

THE CRYSTAL 💎 GEM

The Crystal Gem is the most precious crystal in all of the Kingdom of Fairies, because it carries all the goodness and kindness of the fairies! It is shaped like a heart, on which Blossom's picture is etched. It is preserved in the trunk of the seven virtues (which holds six other trunks in itself). The last of which, the smallest, is made of crystal and fairy silver and holds the Crystal Gem.

Trunk of
Strength

Trunk of
Courage

Trunk of
Generosity

AND ITS STORY

The first trunk is made of gold and contains one made of copper . . . then one of bronze . . . then one of steel . . . one of silver . . . one of rosewood . . . and lastly, the smallest chest is the one made of crystal and fairy silver and it holds the Crystal Gem.

The virtues represented by the Seven Trunks are: strength, courage, generosity, optimism, hope, kindness, and goodness.

The closer you get to the source of evil the heavier the Crystal Gem becomes.

Trunk of
Optimism

Trunk
of Hope

Trunk of
Kindness

Trunk of
Goodness

A THOUSAND HAPPY THOUGHTS

Blossom clapped her hands, and seven fairies appeared carrying a metal chest.

It was the Trunk of the Seven Virtues!

I opened each of the six trunks . . . one of GOLD, one of copper, one of BRONZE, one of steel, one of SILVER, and one of rosewood . . .

Then with trembling paws I lifted the last tiny CRYSTAL chest. Inside I found the CRYSTAL GEM! Its pure light lit up the whole room! In fact, it was so bright I had to close my eyes so I wasn't blinded by it! Yikes!

As I lifted the gem, the sound of a thousand happy thoughts filled the air. What a powerful stone!

Blossom put her hand on my shoulder, "Dear friend," she said, "you truly are our BRIGHT GUARDIAN. Today you have been entrusted with an ENORMOUSE RESPONSIBILITY. The Crystal Gem is extremely powerful and holds all of our fairy powers. Unfortunately, if it gets lost or destroyed or worse, if it ends up in evil hands . . . our Kingdom will be destroyed forever."

A CHILL ran down my fur. The fate of the whole kingdom was in my paws! I was a nervous wreck.

To make matters even worse, Clever Chameleon pulled me aside to warn me about the evil allies of WITHER who would be tracking my every move . . .

HOLEY CHEESE BALLS, HOW TERRIBLY TERRIFYING!

Even though I was **shaking** like a leaf, I tried to keep it together. "Um, so where do I need to bring this Crystal Gem?" I asked in my most calm voice.

Clever Chameleon shook his head, "There is only one person who can tell you:

Mel the Magnificent

and his **Ball of Marvels**! You will leave at once for Sparkle Rock Castle with the helidragon."

"I'll go, too, and keep an eye on him!" Bluewing added.

"If he goes, I'm going! I need to takes notes on what happens," Scribblehopper insisted.

I knew the mini-dragon and the frog would probably get on my

Mel the
Magnificent

NERVES, but I was relieved I would not be alone. Scary missions are even scarier when there's no one to hear you scream! But just as I made my way to the helidragon the castle **alarm horns** began to sound.

"DANGER! DAAAAANGER! THE DARKSHADOW IS AT THE DOORRRRSSS!"

the lookouts called.

Squeak, poor us, it took no time for it to reach us!

Immediately, everyone in the room flew into a panic.

"WE'RE DONE FOR!" they cried.

But Clev got control. The chameleon struck his cane on the ground three times and ordered,

"SILEEEEENCE!"

A LIGHTNESS SPELL!

The chameleon continued, "Inhabitants of the Kingdom of Fantasy, please listen. All is not lost! The only hope for saving the Crystal Castle is to move it immediately to the Bright Mountains! The **Darkshadow** has not reached there yet!"

Then he turned to Blossom and asked, "My Queen, I know that you are **EXHAUSTED**, but do you feel capable of carrying out the most difficult spell of your life . . . the lightness spell?"

She responded decidedly, "Yes, if all the fairies of the kingdom unite their wands with me around the Crystal Gem . . . we can do it!

The fairies all gathered around the **CRYSTAL GEM**, pointed their wands at it, and all sang together . . .

The Lightness Spell

We unite our wands most secure.
They are many, perfect, and pure!
Our hearts we unite,
A treasure so precious and dear.
Our hearts are so light,
Like friends' smiles so sincere.
Light and soft the castle will be,
It holds our greatest gift you see . . .
The treasure is the queen of all,
and little Winglet adored and small!
As light as a cloud,
may Crystal Castle become.
And in a flap of a wing,
we will fly toward the sun!

A fountain of bright sparkles flowed from wands that had united in one great column of light and that rose toward the sky.

Then suddenly, the sparks stopped and for a moment *silence* fell over the great Ceremony Room.

Everyone looked around in astonishment . . .

What next?

I'm flying!

Helppp!

Hee, hee, hee!

Suddenly, the castle began to **tremble** and **shake**. First right, then left until finally . . . it lifted from the ground, as **light** as a crystal butterfly!

Then everything in the **CASTLE** began to float weightlessly. Chairs, plates, utensils, books, pillows, and beds, too . . .

We even lifted up into the **air**!

Help!

Oops!

Am I flying?

Croak!

NOT VERY BRIGHT!

Blossom urged me to leave. "Please go before it's too late!" she cried.

All of the inhabitants of the castle stared at me expectantly. This was my **big** moment. I had to show everyone I was **courageous** enough to get the job done.

"No p-problem," I stuttered. Then I tried to bow before the queen, but I ended up doing a very awkward **somersault** instead.

Everyone in the crowd began to whisper, "The **BRIGHT GUARDIAN** isn't very **bright**!"

Oh, how humiliating!

Next I tried to grab the **CRYSTAL GEM**,

Oops!

but it slipped through
my paws and my head
hit the ceiling.

Here it is!

KABANG!

I heard the crowd
whisper again, "Yep,
he's a bit of a dim bulb, that Bright Guardian."

Finally, I managed to grab the gem, and I stuffed
it in a silk bag that I hung around my neck for
safekeeping. I said good-bye to Blossom and all
of the Fairy Court and floated over
to the dragon landing pad. Little did I know, the
lightness spell didn't work at the landing pad and
suddenly I hit the ground with a thud.

OUCH!

I heard the crowd whisper once again, "Hmmm,
he's dim, very dim."

Embarrassed, I climbed into the cabin and the
helidragon took off.

The helidragon took off like a **SHOT**.

I turned back and watched the Crystal Castle *flying* away.

Even though everyone was picking on me, I hoped they

had a safe trip to the Bright Mountains.

Suddenly, as he flew, the helidragon called out, *"Hang on tiiiiight!"*

Then he **DARTED** forward and before I could say "squeak" I was floating above

GREEN COUNTY!

We passed over the circle of the **Twelve Green Guardians**, who immediately opened to let us through, because they already knew of our arrival . . . and in a **FLASH** we were standing before the doors of **Sparkle Rock**!

WELCOME TO SPARKLE ROCK!

A thick cloud of enchanted, light, and **SCENTED FOG** surrounded the bright castle. The fog hid the castle from unwanted enemies. As I approached, the fog suddenly lifted as if by some **SPELL**, and finally I could see before me the light walls of the castle **sparkling** in the sun. The white-and-gold flag of the **BRIGHT EMPIRE** waved from the top of the tallest tower. It was almost like the flag was waving hello to me!

Here's Sparkle Rock!

"Look, Mel increased the amount of MAGIC FOG! That means that danger also threatens his BRIGHT EMPIRE!" Scribblehopper remarked.

We arrived at the door of Sparkle Rock Castle, where a **KNIGHT** blocked our way. But when he got a good look at me, he **scooped** me up in a bone-crushing hug.

Welcooooome!

Aack!

OOF!

"Welcome, Fearless Knight!" he cried.

Then he added, "Or should I call you BRIGHT GUARDIAN or He Who Must Venture on a Desperate Endeavor and No One Knows If He Will Return or Die?

I am **happy** to see you, even if I fear it's not for long!"

It was my dear friend Ranger, the Ghost Guardian!

I tried to fill my friend in on all the training I had done with Clever Chameleon. I told him all about how I achieved the Blue Belt of the Balanced Path, a prestigious honor. The more I talked the more confident I

GHOST GUARDIAN

At first he may seem just like empty armor, but he's not! He became the Magic Guardian of the Bright Empire when Mel gave him life. He guards Sparkle Rock Castle, defending it from intruders. He is a proud knight, and he loves making a good impression. He spends a lot of time shining himself to keep his armor sparkling. He and Geronimo have become great friends!

began to feel. After all, with my new skills I was more prepared than ever before!

Unfortunately, when I finished speaking the GHOST GUARDIAN was staring at me with pity in his eyes. "I hate to burst your bubble, friend," he began. "But I've seen many aspiring heroes who were convinced they could beat it . . . but they were all sucked up by the Darkshadow."

I turned pale. "Umm, they were sucked up, you say? By the Darkshadow? What exactly do you mean by 'they were SUCKED UP'?"

The Ghost Guardian realized that he had said too much and stopped himself. "Um, well, let's just pretend I didn't say anything. I didn't mention anything about fallen heroes or being sucked up by the

DARKSHADOW

or, er, **Mel the Magnificent** will explain everything," he muttered.

GOOD-BYE, SO LONG, SEE YOU LATER!

At that point I was really thinking of doing an about-face, of turning back, you know, kicking up my paws and skipping out of there. Who wants to get **sucked** up by a Darkshadow . . . or a light shadow . . . or any shadow for that matter! Holey cheese balls, my whiskers were trembling with fright!

I turned to Scribblehopper, hoping he could **calm** me down. "Twisted cattails! Did you hear that? How am I going to take on the Darkshadow? I'm not a hero. I'm a total **'fraidy mouse**! Maybe I should just leave now!" I wailed, turning toward the door.

The frog grabbed me by the tail and **YANKED** hard. "Forget it, Guardian! You have no choice!

It's your job!" he croaked harshly.

Bluewing the mini-dragon bit my ear, yelling, "Pull yourself together, Defender! If you don't I'm going to call CLEVER CHAMELEON. You can't refuse your **mission**! Remember that you promised to have **courage** and to honor the Blue Belt and . . ."

"Oh, please don't tell Master Chameleon!" I interrupted, chewing my whiskers. What could I do? A promise was a promise. I had to try my best even if I ended up a (gasp!) dead rat!

Good-bye, so long!

You can't back out now!

I turned decisively toward Ranger, the Ghost Guardian. "Take me to

I squeaked.

Ranger turned on the metal heels of his armor, squeaking like an old **rusty door**, and headed inside Sparkle Rock Castle. But instead of taking us to Mel's quarters, he went down a secret **PASSAGE** and went lower and lower and lower . . . down the **strangest** stairs I had ever seen!

It was the Chatterly Stairway!

WHO DARES DISTURB ME?

Those strange stairs seemed to never end! And since they were magic stairs in a **magic** castle that belonged to a real wizard, they kept moving, **revealing** new stairs and new passageways. As we walked, the stairs began to **chuckle**. Ha, ha, ha! Ho, ho, ho! Hee, hee, hee! **HOW strange!**

Meanwhile, as we went downward and then upward on those magic stairs, I could hear some **strange organ music**. It sounded like a **waterfall** . . . and a herd of **GALLOPING** unicorns . . . and a **FIRE-BREATHING** dragon all at the same time!

Where was the music coming from?

The Ghost Guardian saw my **PUZZLED** expression and pointed to a large oak door. "In case you're wondering, the music is coming from there. Behind the door is the **MAGIC FOG FACTORY**. For a few days now, Mel has been locked in there making an endless supply of magic fog," he explained.

Then he lowered his voice and whispered, "Based on how the *Magnificent* is playing, I would say that the situation is serious, really serious. If I were you, I'd be very careful not to upset him."

I knocked on the door and entered. What an incredible sight!

I found myself in an **ENORMOUSE** room full of strange machines and equipment. In the center, Mel the Magnificent was seated before a giant **organ** with golden pipes. He was banging away at the keys. The more he hit them, the more FOG came out of the GOLDEN pipes.

"Ahem, Mr. Magnificent, um, sorry to disturb you . . ." I began, hoping against hope he wouldn't be too upset.

He stopped playing suddenly, finishing with a dark ominous chord.

BAM! BAM! BAM!

Instantly, the **puffs** of fog stopped. Mel threw his hands in the air and shrieked, "Who dares to disturb me when I'm creating my magic music? Who?

Who? Who? I gave specific orders that I didn't want to be disturbed!"

With a **trembling** voice I babbled, "Umm . . . actually it's me, the Bright Guardian."

At those words, Mel turned around. When he saw it was me, he gave me a warm wizardly hug. "For all the *magic wands*, you should have said it was **you**! I've been waiting for you!"

I was waiting for you!

Argh!

Then he looked me up and down. "So I hear you've been trained by MASTER CHAMELEON. Who knows, maybe you're not a hopeless case after all. Anyway, we'll soon find out. A dangerous mission awaits. If you manage to come back alive, then you will have become a **TRUE HERO**. And if not, well, then I guess you're still a **hopeless case**."

My fur turned **beet red**. But I still needed to ask Mel some questions about my upcoming journey. Before I could begin, though, he interrupted me.

"So let me guess, you're here to ask for my help. Isn't that always the case? As soon as there's a problem everyone comes to me. Mel this, Mel that — seriously it's enough to drive a

WIZARD up the wall!" he complained.

After ranting and raving for **ten hours** (well, okay, maybe it wasn't that long) he suddenly announced, "Oh, you almost made me forget, it's **teatime**!" He waved his wand and in a flash a table covered with a white tablecloth, a china **tea set**, a **silver tray** full of pastries, and two stuffed armchairs appeared!

137

THE MAGIC
FOG FACTORY

It seemed like a pretty *odd* time to be drinking tea, considering we were in the middle of a serious crisis, but Mel insisted.

"You are wrong, Mouse," he lectured. "It's exactly when the situation is **SERIOUS** that you should stop and REFLECT calmly. And a nice cup of tea is just what we need."

Mel began sipping his tea and munching on the pastries, so I did the same. As I slurped my tea a sense of calm came over me. When I bit into a cheddar pastry I almost forgot about the SCARY mission ahead of me! Everything really is better with cheddar!

When we had finished eating, I asked Mel if he knew how I could complete my mission.

Mel the Magnificent

Mel the Magnificent, the Great Wizard of Light, is also known as Melvin, M & M, the Wizard with the Wand, the Lord of Eternal Spells, the Protector of True Justice, and the Great Solver: He Who Can Find a Solution Even When There's None! That's why the creatures of the Kingdom of Fantasy always ask him for advice. Not much is known about Mel the Magnificent, and he's not talking! He works alone and prefers to be alone (too bad everyone is always asking him for help!). He is incredibly knowledgeable, loves to read books, listen to and play music, and paint. He speaks all the languages of the Kingdom, even the Green Language, which is the language the plants speak.

He nodded, looking off into the distance. But he didn't say a word. I waited and waited. At last, when I was about to pull all my fur out in **FRUSTRATION**, he spoke.

"Of course, there's only one way to know," he said. "Let's consult the Ball of Marvels! But the MAGIC FOG production cannot stop, so as I consult the ball, you will have to play the magic music on the magic organ! Got it, Mouse?"

"Um, but I don't know how to play the organ," I muttered.

Mel lifted his shoulders, unconcerned. "Well, Mouse, there's a *famouse saying* among the wizards of the Bright Empire. Do you know what it is?"

I was silent, and Mel thundered, "If you don't know how to play, you pedal! And do you know why?"

Curious, I **MUTTERED**, "Umm, why?"

Here is the magical . . .

Ball of Marvels!

It was made by Quartzy, the King of the Crystalline Gnomes. It lets you observe everything that happens in the Kingdom.

He chuckled, "You'll **understand** soon!"

He pulled a strange lever at the base of the **organ** . . .

First there was a **grinding** noise. Then a trapdoor opened in the ground

Then a strange — no a really strange — **GOLDEN** bicycle appeared.

Mel exclaimed, "Since you don't know how to play you'll have to **PEDAL**! Better put those paws on the pedal now, or Sparkle

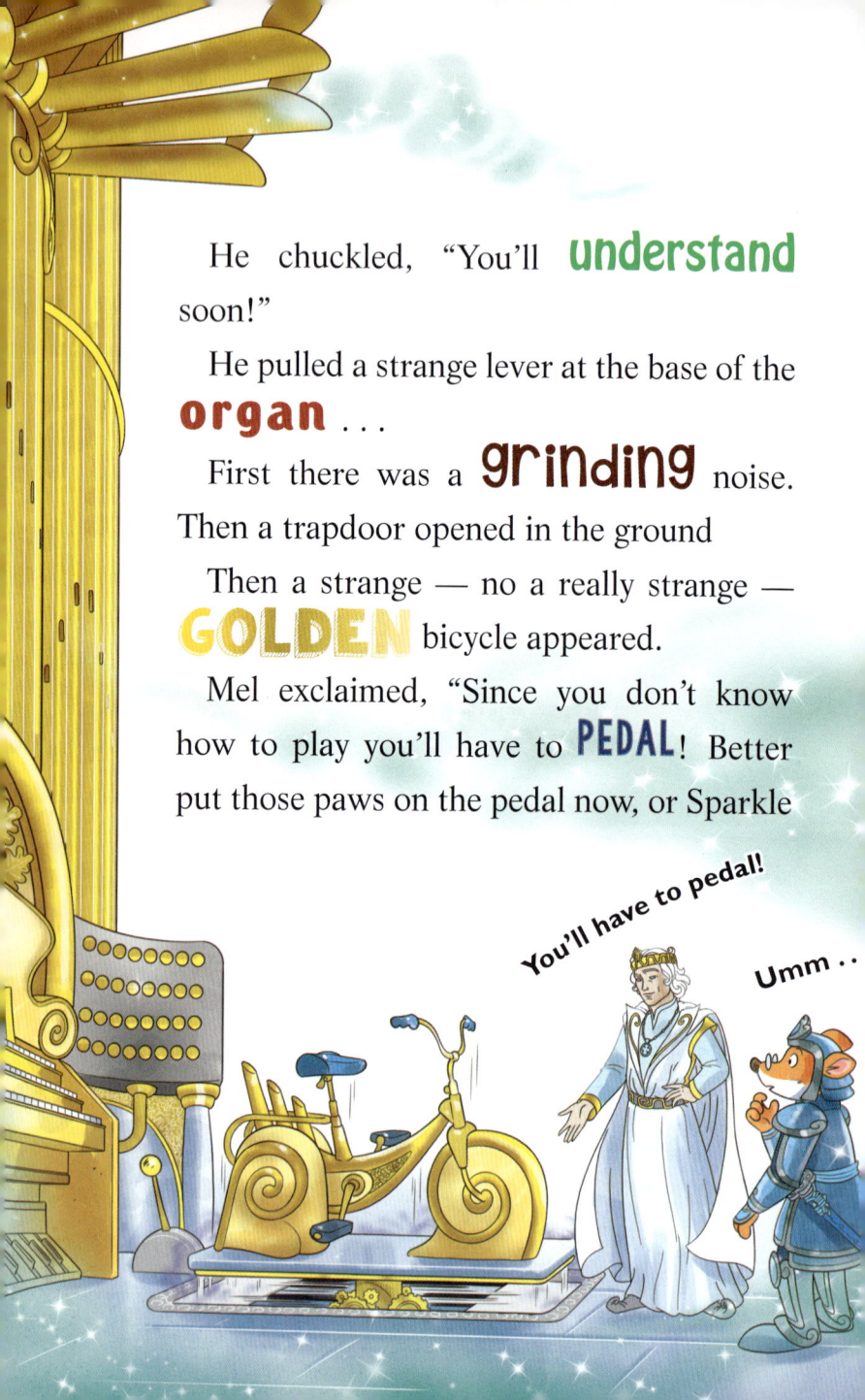

You'll have to pedal!

Umm . .

Rock Castle will be devoured by the Darkshadow!"

Then he left to look in the Ball of Marvels with his **bright cloak** waving behind him, and I climbed on the bicycle and began to pedal.

Argh!

I pedaled . . . and pedaled . . . and pedaled . . . but not a single puff of fog came out of the golden pipes.

SQUEAK, what could I do?

It was then that I heard a **STRANGE** little voice.

"Bright Guardian, you're really not the most athletic mouse are you?" a voice said.

I **jumped**. Who was that?

I looked around with my eyes **wide**

open, but I didn't see anyone. The tiny voice continued with a little laugh, "I'm right here in front of you! My name is Mosquitina of the Mosquitonies, first-class Music Elf! I'm the one who runs the Magic FOG Factory. You don't know how to play."

Only then did I see that in front of me there was a tiny creature who looked like a tiny mosquito fairy!

Do! Re! Me! I love to dance and sing!
Do! Re! Me! I can do most anything!

I'm Mosquitina!

"Don't worry," said Mosquitina, "I will help you. I will play the **keys** while you press on the pedal."

Right then the tiny creature began **JUMPING** around on the keys, making happy-sounding music. Finally, tufts of magic fog flew out of the organ **pipes**.

Do! Re! Me! My help is always free!
Do! Re! Me! Come play along with me!

PUFF . . . PUFF . . . PUFF . . .

Mosquitina jumped from one key to the next playing and singing, sometimes **carefree** and **happy**, and other times slow and dreamy.

Meanwhile, I pedaled . . . and pedaled . . . and pedaled . . . and from the golden pipes of that strange organ small tufts of clouds emerged.

I was so excited but Mosquitina shook her head. "This MAGIC FOG isn't enough to even hide the moat around **Sparkle Rock**, not to mention the entire Kingdom. I will ask my sisters for help."

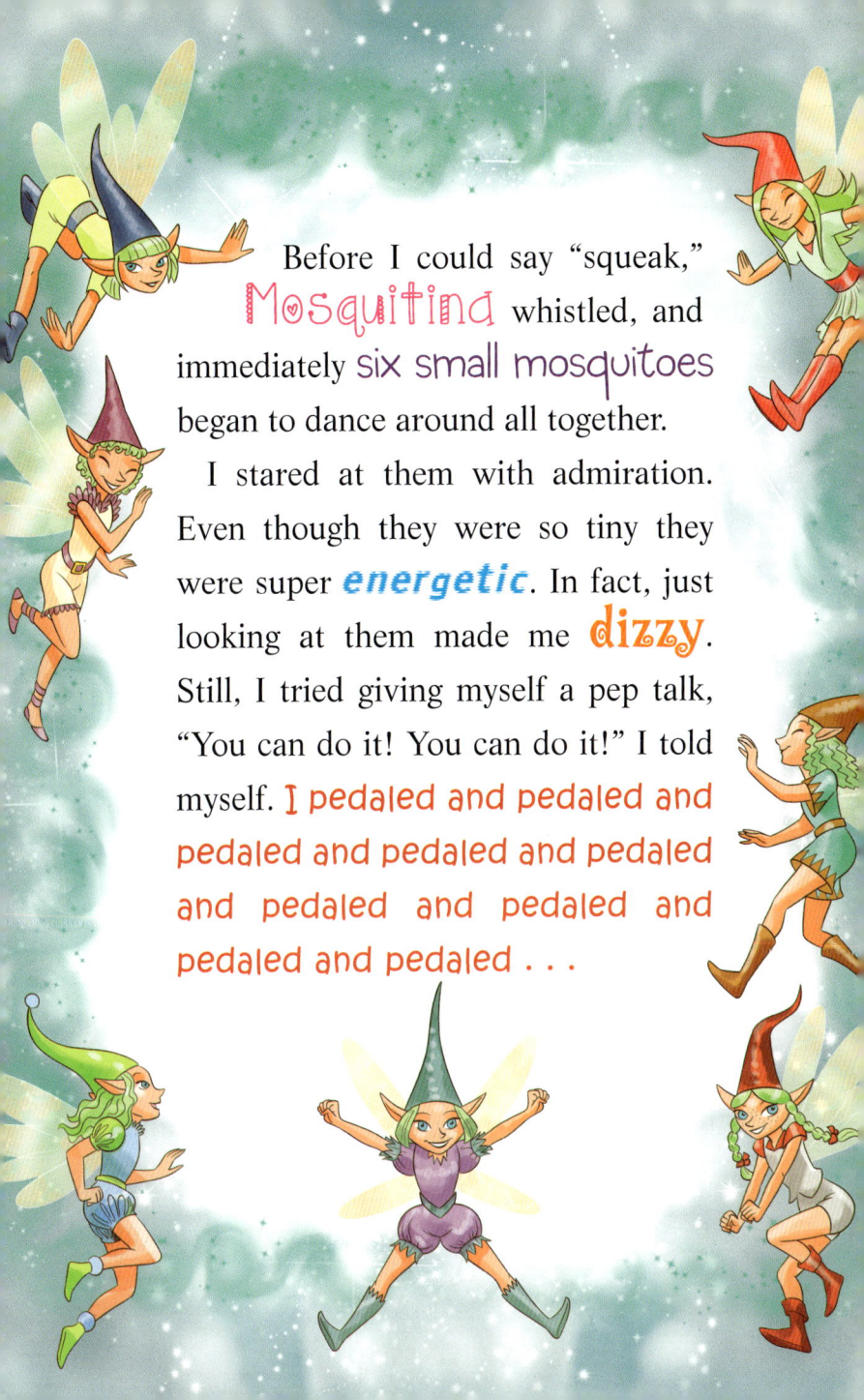

Before I could say "squeak," Mosquitina whistled, and immediately six small mosquitoes began to dance around all together.

I stared at them with admiration. Even though they were so tiny they were super *energetic*. In fact, just looking at them made me dizzy. Still, I tried giving myself a pep talk, "You can do it! You can do it!" I told myself. I pedaled and pedaled and pedaled and pedaled and pedaled and pedaled and pedaled and pedaled and pedaled . . .

Right at that moment, Mel strode back into the room.

"Let's get out of here! It's that GRUMP, Mel!" the mosquitoes cried, slipping out the door before he spotted them.

Mel strode into the room looking pleased. "Well done, MOUSE! Sparkle Rock Castle is completely hidden!" he exclaimed. Then he added, "Were you the one who made all this beautiful MAGIC FOG?

I decided it would be best to tell him the truth, so I admitted that Mosquitina and her sisters helped me.

Mel smiled. "Very good, Mouse. Honesty is the best policy. I imagine that Mosquitina came because my niece, Wolfy, asked her to . . . but that's another story for another time. I came to let you know that the Ball of Marvels has confirmed that the situation is extremely serious!"

Wolfy
and her
magic friends

Owlivia

Wolfy

Roxy

Beartina

Wolfy is Mel's niece. She comes from the Magic Wolf Clan, wizards who can turn into wolves. She goes to Sparkle Rock Magic School with her three friends: Roxy Foxy, Beartina, and Owlivia. They can turn into a fox, a bear, and an owl respectively. The girls are very close friends!

MEL THE MAGNIFICENT'S SECRET

As Mel led me through corridors of the castle, up and down staircases, past little and big rooms, I noticed that the whole place seemed to be entirely empty. Yep, there was not one single fairy or wizard or warlock or creature anywhere in that castle! **HOW STRANGE!** Even though Mel prefers to spend his time alone, the CASTLE is always full of life, and creatures are always coming and going.

When we passed by the rooms of the Magic School I noticed that there was absolute silence. **HOW VERY STRANGE!** Even the front of the Hall of the Great Magic Council was deserted. **HOW VERY, VERY, VERY STRANGE!** What was happening? I was dying to ask Mel but when I started to, he shot me a **LOOK**. Then he held his finger to his lips and motioned for me to be quiet.

In a low voice he cautioned, "Listen, Mouse, even the walls have ears. But don't get your tail in a TWIST. I'll explain everything in bit. Just follow me and keep your snout shut."

At last we stood in front of the Ball of Marvels. Mel raised his magic wand and hit the ball three times. The ball grew ENORMOUSE, opened up, and we went inside!

Tap tap tap

ONE FOR ALL, AND ALL FOR ONE!

As soon as I entered the room my friends ran to greet me. **Wolfy** wrapped me in an enormouse hug. "It's so *good* to see you, Guardian! You are our favorite hero!" she said with a grin. Owlivia, Roxy Foxy, and Beartina followed her lead. And the seven Von Wild brothers *hugged* me, too. Before I knew it I found myself in the center of a massive group hug. Part of me felt great and part of me felt . . . **squished**! Oof!

THE SEVEN VON WILD BROTHERS are the sons of Storm and Sunshine, the wizards of the atmospheric elements. Each one of them possesses a great power.

Luckily, Mel interrupted the **happy** hugging.

Did I mention my rodent bones can be very delicate?

Anyway, where was I? Ah, yes. Mel explained, that I needed to be careful about talking in public about the **Darkshadow** and my mission. "If Blossom has been betrayed in her own palace, that means that Wither could have *spies* anywhere! We sent the students from **Magic School** home, and each wizard returned to their own territory to defend it from the Darkshadow."

"This is a **disaster**!" I squeaked, turning to Mel. "Blossom told me you could advise me. Do you have any ideas?"

Suddenly, I remembered about the Crystal Gem. Maybe that was the answer. I took the sack that held the **CRYSTAL GEM** from around my neck, and pulled it out. A marvelous **golden light** reflected off the walls of the ball and everyone exclaimed in amazement, **"OOOOoooooooooohhhhhh! The Crystal Gem! Incredible!"**

"Blossom told me that in this gem there is a concentrate of all the power and all the goodness of all the **fairies**. It's the only thing that can stop the Darkshadow, but where do I need to take it? I promised the queen that I would help find little **winglet**, even though it may (**SOB!**) kill me," I squeaked.

Right then the Von Wild brothers, Wolfy, and all of her friends gathered around me. "Don't worry, **BRIGHT DEFENDER**, we will come with you," they said.

Mel nodded quietly. "Yes, yes, the mouse cannot go alone. Let's face it, he's not exactly brimming with **courage** and **confidence**!" he smirked.

"Well, I um, I . . ." I was starting to feel insulted.

Mel cut me off. "Ranger, the Ghost Guardian, will come with you for protection. And **Solo, the solitary wizard,** will also go with you, he knows all the mysteries of the Kingdom of Fantasy."

He pointed to a silent young man standing in a corner who was wrapped in a large, **DARK CLOAK**. He bowed his head but didn't say a word.

Solo the wizard

Besides this group, Mel also agreed to let me

bring Scribblehopper and Bluewing. Then he said, "You must go to the **VOLCANO OF THE FIERY ABYSS**. That's where Wither makes the Darkshadow, thanks to Nebula."

I'm coming, too!

Argh!

Suddenly, someone began to **PULL** my whiskers and yell, "Can I come, too?!" It was Mosquitina, the music elf.

NEBULA
THE SHAPE SHIFTER

Nebula, the dark shadow of desperation, is the most evil and wicked of Wither's allies. She created the Darkshadow to wrap the Kingdom of Fantasy in a dense, dark cloud of evil. Nebula is a shape shifter. She can take on any form and trick anyone.

Mel **rolled** his eyes, but in the end he said, "All right, you can go, too!"

I was wondering how we would all get to the **volcano** when Mel tapped the Ball of Marvels. "This is your mode of transportation," he announced.

Huh? Now I was really confused. Did the ball turn into a **bus**? A magic ball bus?

Mel interrupted my thoughts. "I will tell you all a secret. The Ball of Marvels can become **BIG** or small and fly on command." He touched the ball and sang,

"I can go most anywhere,
it's like I fly right through the air.
I just need a magic spell,
that is clear and sung quite well.
Sing it with a heart so true,
with feelings that come just from you.
But if sincere you cannot be . . .
Beware! Trouble you will see!"

THE SECRET OF THE
BALL OF MARVELS

The Ball of Marvels is a powerful ball of the purest crystal that lets you see everything that happens in the Kingdom of Fantasy. It is also an extraordinary mode of transportation that can fly you instantly to any point in the kingdom.

To activate it you must position yourself between the four dragons that hold up the ball and you must sing the Ball Chant. But beware: The chant must be sung by one with a pure heart or there may be deadly consequences!

DO, RE, MI!

Mel handed me a scroll with the chant printed on it. "Don't forget, Mouse, you need to sing it with a pure heart or you're doomed!" he warned.

I blinked. Did I have a pure heart? I always tried to do the right thing. Well, except for the time I pretended I had a **stomachache** during my school soccer tournament. The other team was **huge**! I was scared for my life!

I was still thinking about the game as I practiced my scales with Mosquitina.

Finally, after **HOURS** and **HOURS** and **HOURS** of practice, the music elf declared we were all in perfect pitch. I was relieved. Don't get me wrong, I'm not tone deaf, but you won't catch me on *New Mouse City's Got Talent* any time soon.

Before we left, Mel reminded us again to sing with a **pure** heart. Then he handed me a pair of **strange** glasses. "These are

ENCHANTED GLASSES,"

he said. "You may need them. Watch out for what you think you see. Not everything is as it seems!"

Eventually, Mosquitina gave us a "**la**" and we began to sing with one single voice. Within minutes, the eyes of the four dragons that held the ball **LIT UP**. Strong rays of blue light shot out from the dragons' eyes, and we were surrounded by a **magic light**.

"Have a good trip!" Mel called. Then I felt a really strong tingling sensation from the tip of my ears to the tip of my tail . . . there was a flash of light and . . . **POOF!**

We were transported far . . .

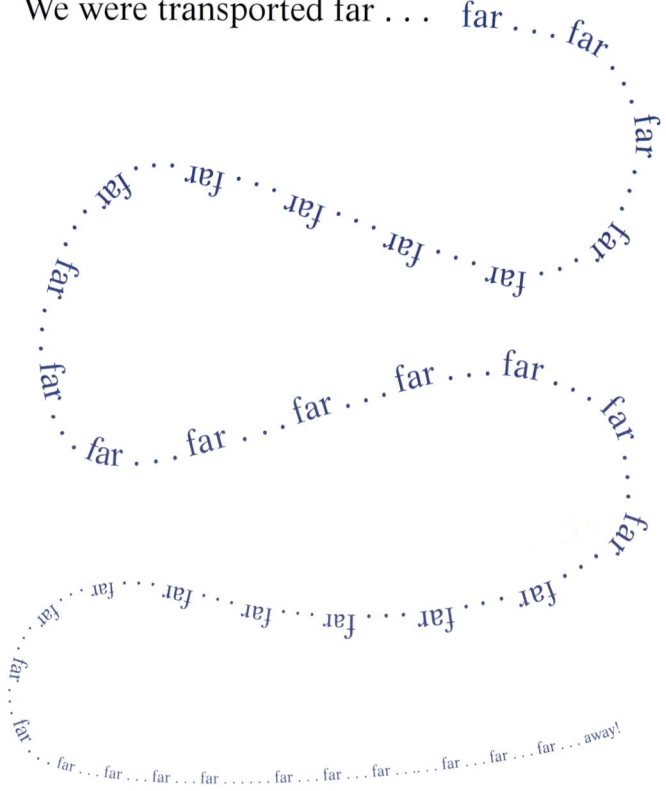

far . . . away!

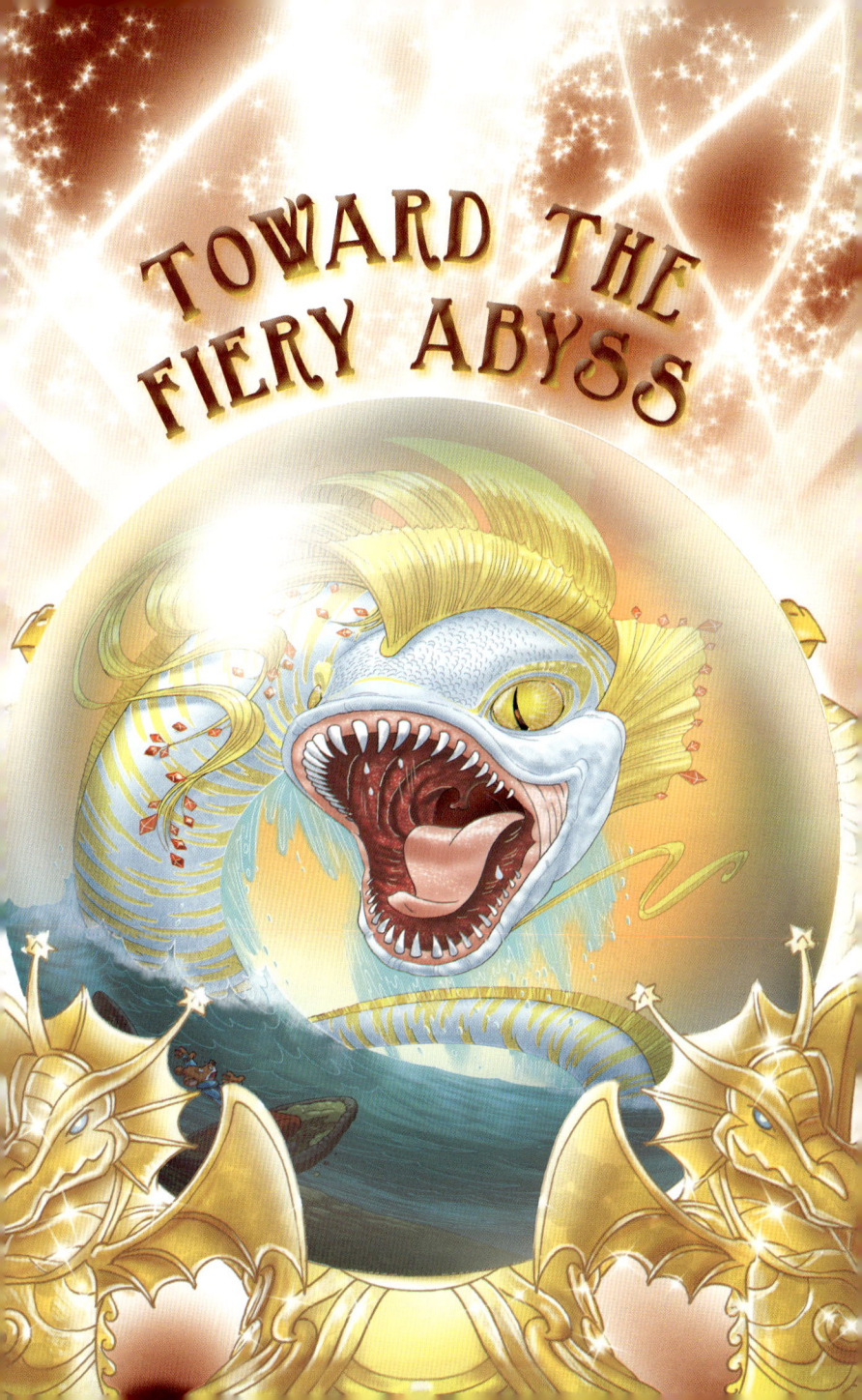

TOWARD THE FIERY ABYSS

HOLEY CHEESE BALLS, WHERE ARE WE?

I stood up. Yes, my tail was bruised, but I was alive! I stumbled on my feet.

First I **checked** to see if I was all in one piece (*tail, ears, and whiskers included!*). Then I checked that the **CRYSTAL GEM** was still in the little sack around my neck.

Only after that did I look around as I rubbed my head (*luckily I was wearing armor!*). I thought I would be at the top of the **VOLCANO** of the Fiery Abyss, but instead, I just saw lots of water and a dense, grayish **FOG** that wound slowly along like a pack of snakes. Brrr!

"**HOLEY CHEESE BALLS!**" I exclaimed.

"Where is the ?"

Desperation Swamp

is a vast expanse of water surrounded by patches of grayish fog where the air smells of rotten algae and putrid mud. Stay clear of this place because if you stay here too long desperation will come over you!

It's so desolate!

The Ghost Guardian muttered gloomily, "I think we're lost forever in this **Swamp**! I knew we shouldn't trust magical modes of transportation. A tried-and-true method would have been better, like a good old **dragon**! Or why not even a unicorn . . . Or even just by foot!"

I was worried. "Maybe I'm just a **horrible** singer. Or maybe I really am tone deaf. Or maybe my heart isn't pure enough!" I whined.

Mosquitina **PULLED** my whiskers. "Don't be silly, Guardian, your voice was **pitch perfect**!" she assured me, crossing her little mosquito hands. "Mosquito's honor!"

Wolfy nodded in agreement. "She's right. And if your heart wasn't **pure**, Blossom wouldn't have chosen you for this mission."

At that moment, I noticed Roxy Foxy staring at the others intently. "Someone here might very

well be the problem," she muttered softly. "I wonder if there is a **traitor** among us."

Croak! Croak! Croak!

"That's enough **CHATTER**!" Scribblehopper insisted, jumping up. He looked around and, **clapping** one webbed hand to his head, he announced, "I know where we are! If my frog memory is right, we are in **Saliva Swamp** . . . Or maybe this is **Buggy Bog** or maybe . . . I have no idea!"

DESPERATION SWAMP

S olo, who up to that point hadn't said one word, announced sternly, "Frog, this is Desperation Swamp. I can tell because of the **rotten algae stench** and **putrid mud**. If we stay here too long, *desperation* will come over us, and we won't be able to **MOVE**. Let's get out of here!"

Let's go!

What a sad place!

He grabbed his satchel and yelled, "Follow me! I'll get us out of here, but we have to hurry!"

I quickly followed Solo, but every step I took my heart became sadder, my steps were **heavier**, and the bag with the crystal gem around my neck felt like a ten-ton boulder. Now I knew why they called it Desperation Swamp! Vultures circled above our heads singing a CREEPY song.

Come on, let's get out of here!

Follow me!

"FROM THE SWAMP YOU'LL
NEVER GET FREE,
AND FOOD FOR US VULTURES
YOU WILL SOON BE!
MANY HAVE COME, MANY HAVE TRIED
WHERE'D THEY END UP? JUST
CHECK OUR INSIDES!"

As we walked, Solo yelled out instructions. "Don't Stop! Don't listen to the vultures! Don't walk in zigzags! Don't look down! Don't look up!"

Thundering cattails! What was next? **Don't breathe?!**

BALD-HEADED VULTURES

They are the wicked vultures of the Kingdom of Fantasy. Their heads have no feathers, and they spend their days flying over Desperation Swamp in search of new prey!

Scribblehopper was the only one who looked at ease. He jumped here and there, playing in the mud. Croak!

"Why is everyone so worried?" he snorted. "It's just a little mud! Ribbit! Ribbit!"

Ribbit!

How strange!

I was surprised that my friend didn't seem to sense the **evilness** of that horrid swamp. But I told myself it was just that he was a frog. Don't all frogs love swamps?

Several times Scribblehopper offered to carry the pouch with the Crystal Gem. He didn't seem tired and hopped along like he didn't have a care in the world. How strange.

Still, I was too **exhausted** to think about it.

As we walked, Owlivia, Wolfy, and Roxy Foxy chatted quietly. "I wish we could use our magic. Then we could escape this place," Owlivia said sadly.

We can't use magic here!

Solo nodded. "The witch would definitely find us if we used magic," he agreed.

We were forced to walk . . . and walk and . . . and walk . . . and walk and . . . and walk and . . . and walk and . . . and walk and . . . and walk and walk . . . and walk . . . and walk . . . and walk . . . and walk . . . and walk and . . . and walk and . . . and walk and . . . and walk and . . . and walk and . . . and walk walk . . . and walk . . . and walk . . . and walk . . . and walk . . . and walk and . . . and walk and . . . and walk and . . . and walk and . . . and walk and . . . and walk walk . . . and walk . . . and walk . . . and walk . . . and walk . . . and walk . . . and walk and walk and . . . and walk and . . . and walk and . . . and walk and . . . and walk and . . . and walk and and walk . . . and walk . . . and walk . . . and walk . . . and walk . . . and walk . . . and walk . . . and walk and . . . and walk and . . . and walk and . . . and walk and . . . and walk and . . . and walk . . . and walk . . . and walk . . . and walk . . . and walk . . . and walk . . . and walk and . . . and walk and . . . and walk and . . . and walk and . . . and walk and . . . and walk . . . and walk . . . and walk . . . and walk . . . and walk . . . and walk . . . and walk and . . . and walk and . . . and walk and . . . and walk and . . . and walk . . . and walk and . . . walk . . . and walk . . . and walk . . . and walk . . . and walk . . . and walk . . . and walk and . . . and walk and . . . and walk and . . . and walk and . . . and walk and . . . walk and . . . and walk . . . and walk . . . and walk . . . and walk . . . and walk . . . and walk and . . . walk and . . . and walk and . . . and walk and . . . and walk and . . . and walk and . . . and walk . . . and walk . . . and walk . . . and walk . . . and walk . . . and walk . . . and walk . . . and walk . . . and walk and . . . and walk and . . . and walk and . . . and walk and . . . and walk and . . . and walk and and walk . . . and walk . . . and walk . . . and walk . . . and walk . . . and walk . . . and walk and . . . and walk and . . . and walk and . . . and walk and . . . and walk and . . . and walk and . . . walk . . . and walk . . . and walk . . . and walk . . . and walk . . . and walk . . . and walk . . .

AnD finally we reacheD the banks of a sea, beyonD which we coulD see the Fiery Abyss . . .

THE FIERY ABYSS!

Solo signaled for us to stop. He pointed to an island in the distance, where a really tall volcano was shooting streams of lava. *Dense smoke* that smelled like **rotting** fish polluted the **air**.

"Well, I hate to tell you, Mouse, but that's where we need to go," Solo announced. "That is the legendary

FIERY ABYSS!"

I gulped as my knees **buckled** in fright. "Squeak! I want to live!" I sobbed uncontrollably.

Bluewing **smacked** me with his wing. "Pull yourself together . . . or at least pretend!" he whispered in my ear.

I swallowed hard as I stared at a stretch of

Have some courage!

restless **black sea** with tall waves that separated us from the island.

"How will we get to the island? I don't see any **boats**! And I don't want to rust my armor," the Ghost Guardian remarked.

Scribblehopper had an idea. It seemed Ophidian, a legendary sea serpent with silver-blue scales, lived in the sea. "If we can find him, maybe he will help us get to the island."

I was very worried.

"If Ophidian is a legendary creature, how will we find him? And how will we convince him to **TAKE US**? But most of all, are we sure that he really exists?" I squeaked.

Scribblehopper crossed his arms, offended.

OPHIDIAN

Near the island of the Fiery
Abyss there is a legendary sea serpent,
Ophidian, who circles the island day and night
to warn wayward travelers. No one can reach the
island without drowning in the thick waters that
surround it or roasting in the rivers of lava that fall
from the volcano. Ophidian takes his job very seriously.
He is Blossom's loyal friend, and he belongs to the
family of the Winged Ones. He has golden eyes,
and his fins and whiskers are pure gold . . .
and he loves mussels!

"Are you doubting my words?" he croaked.

I quickly apologized as I explained that sometimes legends don't always tell the truth, the whole truth, and nothing but the truth.

HUMPH! HMM . . .

WHO KNOWS!

Just then Roxy Foxy clapped her hands together. "I have an idea!" she shouted. "If he likes **mussels**, maybe we could lure him over with one."

"That's a great idea!" Wolfy, Beartina, and Owlivia cheered. "We call him out of the sea with a **mussel**, and that way we can talk to him!"

I looked around and muttered, "But there aren't any **mussels** here."

The girls shrugged. "No

problem. We can make a fake **SUPER-MUSSEL SHELL**! Come on everyone, let's get started!"

We **worked** all day to make a **FAKE MUSSEL SHELL** that really looked real!

Still, the Ghost Guardian shook his head. "Something is missing," he observed. "I know! You need a mollusk that's orange and appetizing! I think the Defender would be perfect!"

"Why me?" I protested.

What a brilliant idea!

Let's get to work!

But everyone agreed I was the perfect mouse for the job because I would tremble in fear just like a **quivering** mollusk. **HOW embarrassing!**

Nevertheless, I let them wrap me up in one of the Von Wild brother's **orange** cloaks. I tucked myself into the mussel, and waited for *Ophidian* . . .

I waited all night,
trembling with real
fear, until suddenly at
dawn I heard a strange
sound in the waves,
I turned and . . .

PLEASE DON'T EAT ME!

An **enormouse** creature with white scales emerged from the DARK sea. He seemed to stare at me like he was starving! I tried to free myself from my mussel **costume**, but I had trembled so much that I was **trapped** in the orange fabric like a fly in a spiderweb!

"Please don't eat me!" I shrieked.

"I'M A MOUSE, NOT A MOLLUSK!"

Ophidian looked at me with a quizzical air. "Maybe you're a mouse, or maybe a mollusk. But you SMELL like a mollusk, you're orange like a mollusk, you shake like a mollusk . . . so I say you're a mollusk! Now stop making such a fuss! I'm going to eat you and that's that!" he insisted.

He opened his giant mouth and was about to swallow me whole when I finally managed to draw my sword and . . .

Riiiiip!

I cut open my disguise from the inside and jumped out, yelling, "Look, I have ears like a mouse, a tail like a mouse, paws like a mouse, and even whiskers like a mouse. Make no mistake, I'm a mouse!"

He seemed confused. "How strange. I've never seen a mouse who wears armor and smells just like a mollusk," he mumbled.

I held up my paws. "Please, don't eat me! I'm the Bright Defender! Blossom sent me, I have a **mission** to carry out!" I cried desperately.

Right then my friends came to my defense. They explained that I really was the Bright Guardian and together we were called the **GEM TEAM**.

Too bad the serpent was not convinced. "Well, that's all very interesting," he mused. "And I've heard talk of the **GEM TEAM**, a group chosen by Blossom, led by the **BRIGHT GUARDIAN**. But if you are telling the truth, where is the gem?"

Well, this was the moment of truth. I had been instructed never to show anyone the **CRYSTAL GEM**. If I did, it could mean the destruction of the entire Kingdom of Fantasy! So I took a deep breath and said, "I cannot show it to you or anyone else. I **promised** I would never endanger it."

TEST? WHAT TEST?

I was sure that Ophidian would devour me at any moment! And I could already imagine his enormouse teeth **BITING** through my tail. But instead, after a long while, I heard a strange grumbling . . .

HMMPH . . . HMMMPH . . . HRMPH . . .

Then I heard something very much like a roar.

HA, HA, HA! HA, HA, HA, HA, HA, HA, HA!

But it wasn't a roar. It was Ophidian's powerful laugh!

As soon as he calmed down, the serpent exclaimed,

"Ho, ho, ho! Ha, ha, ha! Hee, hee, hee! Hi, hi, hi! Hu, hu, hu!

I haven't laughed that much in years—no, in centuries, no, in millennia!"

Then he became **serious** again. "But I respect you, Mouse, because even if you were scared, you passed the test," he added.

My eyes flew open. "Test? What test?" I squeaked.

He *smiled*. "I believe you. You are the Bright Guardian! Only the true Guardian would have refused to show me the **CRYSTAL GEM** and risked his own life to defend it! So I will not eat you. It's your **lucky** day!" He chuckled.

I let out a loud sigh. Then I gathered my courage and asked, "Can you give us a lift? We need to reach the **FIERY ABYSS**."

Ophidian slithered quickly up to the shore. "All aboard!" he yelled, sticking out his **golden** fin as if it were a ladder, so that we could all get on.

We climbed up onto his back and then

held on tight. It wasn't easy. Sea serpents are **SLIPPERY**!

"Hold on! We're off to the **FIERY ABYSS**!" Archie called.

And that's how, with wind in our whiskers, we

We're off to the Fiery Abyss!

sailed on the back of Ophidian as Solo **played** his guitar and sang a song he dedicated to the great sea creature. Maybe, just maybe, we could

save the

Kingdom of Fantasy after all!

THE SECRET OF THE SEVEN WALLMARES

Ophidian *sliced* through the waves as he swam superfast. He moved his enormouse fins and created a wake of  behind him just like a boat.

Once in a while a wave that was higher than the others came along and washed over us, **DRENCHING** us with water.

Besides being scared half to death I also got quite **seasick**! Oh, what a nightmare!

Eventually, the Island of the Fiery Abyss grew closer and closer and closer. Right away my heart began pounding at the terrifying sight.

THUMP! THUMP! THUMP!

The beach was made of thick sand as **DARK** and **slimy** as a sewer rat! And the stinky smoke from the volcano left me gagging for fresh air. (Not a good feeling when you are already seasick!)

Finally, Ophidian pulled up onto the beach and I rolled off his back, **trembling** on the ground. Cheese niblets, I was a **frazzled**, **furry** mess!

Then I noticed the ground was **shaking** beneath my paws.

Brrrr, I'm freezing!

It was an **EARTHQUAKE** so strong I had trouble staying on my feet!

Scribblehopper croaked, "Hmmm, if my frog memory serves me right, now that we've landed on the Island of the **FIERY ABYSS** there's only one little thing we need to do, one **minor** detail, just a little nothing, a miniscule task, a **teensy-tiny** particularity really . . ." His voice trailed off.

"What?! What is it?!" I squeaked, impatiently.

Finally, after a **billion** years (maybe it was only a few minutes, but it felt like forever!), the frog explained that we needed to climb over something called the Seven Wallmares. They were called **Wallmares** because they were nightmarish walls.

I turned **PALE**. "'Nightmares' in what way?"

Solo, who knows all the mysteries of the kingdom, said, "They are **REALLY, REALLY DANGEROUS**! The first wall is made up of super-stinky swamp-troll mud. It's guarded by **super-stinky** trolls. And there are six other scary walls. Each one is worse than the last!"

Scribblehopper stared at me with his eyes *half* open. "Hmm, this sounds way, way too scary. I'm thinking we should give up. What do you think, Defender, are you ready to go *HOME*?"

Before I had a chance to answer, the frog turned to the others and croaked, "The Defender said that we won't be able to get past the **wallmares** and we should all go back *home*! Too bad, we lost! The Kingdom of Fantasy is lost!"

I couldn't believe my ears. What was Scribblehopper talking about? I didn't say we should leave. I mean, don't get me wrong. I was **SCARED**, but I wasn't ready to give up on the Kingdom of Fantasy. I had promised Queen Blossom I would help.

Scribblehopper **huffed** when I told him

I wanted to continue with the mission. "Fine," he muttered. "We'll keep going."

I was so **SURPRISED** my old friend wasn't being more supportive. But I didn't have time to stop and think about it. Solo was already headed *down* the path that led to the first wall, and I raced to keep up.

The **stench** from the first wall nearly knocked me off my feet.

"I think I have an idea," Foxy proposed. "We can use our capes to protect us against the **disgusting** troll sneezes."

When she saw me holding my nose she laughed. "Sorry, Defender. The capes won't keep the **stench** away, but they're better than nothing."

The **stink** was enough to make a grown mouse cry! Oh, why did I not think to bring a good pair of **nose plugs** with me on this journey?

As we got closer, a giant wall of putrid green

swamp mud buzzing with thousands of giant BITING horseflies rose in front of us. Even worse (if that's possible!), a row of hideous trolls stared down at us from the top of the wall, letting out torrents of GLOOPY WET sneezes.

Rat-munching rattlesnakes! Didn't anyone ever teach those trolls to use a tissue when you have to SNEEZE?

The First Wallmare: I was still thinking about tissues when Solo screamed, "Here, Mouse, help me use this POINTY tree trunk to break through the wall!"

Together we began battering the wall. With three hard BLOWS we managed to make a humongous crack in the wall. "We did it!" everyone yelled happily, squeezing through the opening.

The trolls, who were disappointed that we managed to pass one of the walls, howled, "You passed this wall but it's the last, the others you

will never pass! You will be stopped, you will be beaten! And at the next wall you'll be eaten!"

We ran away as fast as we could. In the distance we could see the **Second Wallmare**. It was a super-tall wall made of starving carnivorous plants!

Squeak! How would we manage to pass it?

Then Beartina remembered that she had some **HONEY** candies in her pocket and yelled out, "I have an idea! We can feed the plants, and while they're eating we will try passing them!"

The Second Wallmare: Luckily, the carnivorous plants loved the **HONEY** candies, and while they were busy chewing them we managed to pass and climb their **THORNY** braided branches.

Only when we were already at the other side did the plants realize that it was too late to stop us!

We reached the Third Wallmare and I cringed. It was a wall made of spiderwebs, and it was defended by an enormouse **furry, black** spider! The web was supersticky, but we had no choice. We had to crawl under it.

"The Guardian will have to distract the **spiders** to keep them from **attacking** us!" Scribblehopper croaked.

"Why me?" I protested.

But Scribblehopper smirked. "Because you're the **BRIGHT GUARDIAN**! It is your duty!"

The Third Wallmare: Then he added in a **NASTY** tone, "The spiders will find you very tasty, Defender. You're a perfect mouse-sized appetizer!"

I couldn't believe my frog friend was willing to **THROW** me to the sharks, er, I mean spiders, but he was right about one thing: I was the Defender! And so I did my best to distract the spiders. First I did a little dance, then I sang an **annoying** song, then I stuck out my tongue. It worked!

I slipped under the wall at the last second as the spiders crawled after me, furious. "You escaped again, but just you wait. The witches are waiting, so don't be late! They're after your bones! They'll pick you dry! It's the end for you! Good riddance! Good-bye!"

When we reached the next wall I gasped. It was made of bones and surrounded by **WITCHES**!

The Fourth Wallmare: Wolfy took one look at the witches and **clapped** her hands. "I got this one!" she exclaimed, turning to her friends. "Girls, hold up your mirrors. I know how to deal with witches. They are super **VAIN**!"

The four friends stood in front of the wall with their **mirrors** and yelled, "Who wants to take a look? Who is the **ugliest**, most

horrendous, and scariest witch here?"

Immediately the witches began to fight, casting spells on one another as we passed undisturbed through a tiny door!

By the time they realized it, we were already far gone!

They yelled furiously, "You got past, but you'll finish last! Of the black fairies there are thirty-three, and no one is crueler, you shall see! They'll leave it to their violins to make you tremble and erase your grins!"

Before us stood the Fifth Wallmare. It had sharp spires and a swarm of black fairies playing silver violins.

Luckily, Solo had a plan. He led us to a HOLLOW tree that was all twisted up like it had been struck by lightning. "This is the SECRET PASSAGE known only to the Solitary Guardians of the Kingdom of Fantasy," he explained.

He sang three notes of an **enchanted** melody, and a secret passage opened in the middle of the tree trunk! Sweet cheddar cheese rolls! What a welcome sight! Filled with excitement, we raced down a **long, long, long**, dark passageway and in a flash we were on the other side!

The Black Fairies realized we had escaped, and in anger they broke the bows of their violins and screamed.

The **Sixth Wallmare** was exactly as the black fairies described it. It was a wall made of twisted branches. Flapping around the wall were evil-looking black crows with copper beaks. **CAW!**

This time Mosquitina had a plan. "I know what to do," she declared. "We need to sing the **SECRET** lullaby together."

To be honest, I felt a little self-conscious singing, but I did my best to stay in **tune**. And, in the end, the crows fell fast asleep!

We climbed over the wall using a long rope. **Safe!**

The crows woke up and cawed in unison, "**Don't brag about this one, because next time you'll be done! The giants will smash and crush you. And when they finish, you'll be through!**"

The **Seventh Wallmare** was the last and most dangerous one because it was made up of **giants**!

But again, Mosquitina had a plan. "They may be **giants**, but they don't have giant brains. In fact, they're quite dull." Then she flew up to one of the giant's heads.

He was snoozing and she pulled one of his hairs. The giant became **furious** and thought that his neighbor had done it. One moment later the giants all began to **fight** . . .

It's Not Me!

We were so excited. We had passed all the Wallmares. Now there was no other obstacle between us and the Volcano of the Fiery Abyss!

Everyone cheered,

HURRAY FOR THE GEM TEAM!

Hurray!

Yippee!

We did it!

Still, I wasn't sure if I should be **happy** or **TERRIFIED**!

The volcano was super-dangerous. Rivers of hot **lava** were shooting out of it and it let out dense clouds of Darkshadow. **What a terrifying place!**

Worried, I muttered, "Maybe we should hold off on the celebrating. That volcano looks SOOOOOO scary!"

Meanwhile, the Crystal Gem seemed to be getting **HEAVIER** and **HEAVIER** around my neck.

Scribblehopper put a paw on my shoulder and whispered, "Don't worry, Defender! I'm here to *help you*! Your friend Scribblehopper **understands** you. Do you want me to **HeLP** you carry that heavy Crystal Gem? That way you can rest," he offered.

Give it to me!

No, thank you!

I responded **kindly**, "No, thank you, Scribblehopper! I promised Blossom I wouldn't give the **GEM** to anyone and that

I, alone, would take care of it! I can't break my promise."

Scribblehopper huffed. "Whatever, you say."

We continued walking and with every step the Crystal Gem that I carried around my neck became **HEAVIER** and **HEAVIER** . . .

It was right then that a breathless mini-dragon messenger arrived and announced, "Urgent message for the Guardian from the Clever Chameleon!"

And he read:

Careful, Bright Guardian, someone from the Gem Team will betray you! That's why:

1. *Only trust those who are deserving.*

2. *Don't judge those by what they say, but instead by what they do.*

3. *Remember that eyes are the gateway to the soul and they can show you who really stands before you!*

Your master,

CLEVER CHAMELEON

I was **speechless**!

How could one of my friends betray me?

Everyone said, "It's not me, Defender!"

I **LOOKED** them in the eyes one by one.

They all seemed sincere.

But I had to keep in mind what Clever said . . .

I WAS TROUBLED AND THOUGHTFUL . . .

At **sunset** we finally stopped to rest, and I fell right to sleep with a sad heart and my mind full of **heavy thoughts** . . .

BETRAYAAAAL!

At midnight Scribblehopper woke me up. "Betrayaaaaal! Wake up, waaake up, we need to get **OUT** of here, at **ONCE**!" he croaked. "The other members of the team want to betray you!"

"Huh? What? How? When? Why?" I stammered sleepily.

"I heard them with my own ears," the frog

Betrayaaaal!

Huh? What?

insisted. "They were saying that they want to take the **CRYSTAL GEM**."

He continued with a **MOURNFUL** voice, "You're too good, too trusting, too naïve. Basically you're a fool! *Luckily*, I'm here to look out for you. I heard them with my own frog ears. They were having a **SECRET MEETING** to take the Crystal Gem!"

I exclaimed, astonished, "Are you sure? Are you absolutely sure?"

"Are you calling me a liar?" he yelled. "I'm offended. Look, see for yourself!"

He led me behind a cliff where I saw all the members of the Gem Team meeting around a **FIRE**.

The wind brought me a few words of their whispered conversation: pssst . . . weight . . . gem . . . tired . . . Guardian . . . we need to insist . . . secret . . . quickly . . . Nebula . . .

I couldn't understand what they were saying,

and I was going to go to my friends and ask them to explain why they were having this secret meeting, but Scribblehopper held me back.

"Did you hear, Defender? They are **plotting** against you! They want to take the gem! Don't let them see you. We need to get out of here, at once! Come on, this is no time to drag your paws! Remember Clever Chameleon's message? He warned you that someone was out to betray you!"

"But he said 'someone' from the team. Not the whole team," I protested. "I don't want to be alone!"

Still the frog whispered in my ear, "Listen, I am here with you, you're not alone! *Quick*, let's get out of here before they notice!"

And so, with a saddened heart, I abandoned the Gem Team and headed toward the top of the volcano.

We climbed, and climbed, and climbed, and

climbed, and climbed, and I grew more and more discouraged, and more and more tired, and more and more sad and melancholy.

I will help you with the gem!

But Scribblehopper JUMPED around happily. HOW STRANGE! I didn't understand how he could be so *content* about the whole situation when I was so miserable. HOW STRANGE!

As we climbed closer to the top of the volcano it grew even HOTTER. The air BURNED my fur like we were in the middle of the desert in August. I was so hot in my armor even my whiskers were sweating!

The whole time we climbed Scribblehopper kept asking me if I was tired and if he could help me carry the heavy CRYSTAL GEM. "I'm your friend, after all," he croaked. "And friends need to help friends!"

"Thank you, Scribblehopper, but carrying the gem is my task and my task only. I promised Blossom," I replied.

Finally, we arrived at the top of the volcano. I breathed a sigh of relief. I was finally close to completing my mission.

We sat for a moment to catch our breath. Meanwhile, I stared at the burning lava that boiled in the mouth of the VOLCANO.

I turned toward Scribblehopper happily and said, "I'm so glad we almost made it! Soon I will throw the gem into the mouth of the volcano and the Kingdom will be saved!"

"Umm, Guardian, before throwing the gem, do

you want to **eat** something? Or **DRINK** some swamp grass tea?" he responded.

"Thanks, friend, but I'll rest when I've gotten rid of the gem," I said, getting up so I could move closer to the edge of the crater.

Scribblehopper got up, too, and then, who knows how, I *tripped* over the frog's big foot and fell!

I thought I was definitely a goner until right at that instant I managed to grab on to a rock that

was **JUTTING** out. The frog grabbed me by the paw.

"Thanks, Scribblehopper!" I called. "Pull me up!"

But instead of pulling me to safety he yelled, *"Give me the gem, Bright Guardian!"*

HOW STRANGE!

I explained once again that I couldn't give it to him, but he insisted, *"Give me the gem, and if you should fall I will throw it in for you!"*

HOW REALLY STRANGE!

I tried not to look down as I argued with Scribblehopper, my dear old friend. But was he really my friend?

Just then I looked at him right in the **eyes**. At last I understood.

Because staring him in the eyes I saw that they were full of greed ... they weren't the eyes of a friend!!

WHAT A FURRY RAT FOOL!

You!" I squeaked, looking closely at Scribblehopper. "You are the traitor! It was **you** all along!"

Furious, he shouted, "If you don't give me the gem, I will let you fall into **nothingness**!"

I turned and for a moment I saw the bottom of the cliff.

Sour Swiss rolls! Did I mention I have a fear of heights, molten volcanoes, and friends who pretend to be friends but then aren't?

Still I refused to give up the gem, which made Scribblehopper **shriek** with rage, "What a **furry rat fool**!"

As I stared at him everything around Scribblehopper began to slowly disappear and in

Fool!

a few seconds the frog turned into a cloud of *dark smoke*.

Then I saw that it wasn't my dear frog friend at all. It was Nebula!

I yelled, "You were the **TRAITOR**. I mean, you're not Scribblehopper, you're **NEBULA**!"

Right then the hand that was holding me vanished, and I f e l l . . .

As I was falling I squeaked, "HEEEEEEEELP!

HEEEEEEEEEELLLPPPPPP!"

But my words were lost in the wind and I kept falling. I thought that I would get splattered on the ground like **scrambled** mouse. But lucky for me the **enchanted** armor that Clever had given me saved me.

Then, suddenly, I felt **KIND** hands beneath me, and **KIND** voices reassuring me, and **KIND** eyes smiling at me . . . It was my friends! My real friends from the Gem Team who would never have betrayed me!

They all shouted, "Don't be afraid, **BRIGHT GUARDIAN**, we are here to **protect you**!"

They placed me **gently** on the ground. I didn't have one scratch! I hugged them all. "Thank you for saving me!" I squeaked with tears in my eyes.

True friends really are life savers!

A FLASH OF
BLUE LIGHT!

I felt really bad for not having trusted the Gem Team. "I'm sorry, everyone, but when I heard you all talking around the FIRE I thought you were plotting against me. I thought you were planning on stealing the gem," I explained.

They were stunned, and then they all burst out in laughter.

"No, Guardian, we were talking about helping you. You're our friend. We would never do anything to mess up the mission for you."

I sighed. If only I had asked my friends what they were meeting about. Well, there was one lesson I would never forget. Communication is key in any friendship! I was grateful that my real friends forgave me.

That got me thinking about real friends and **fake** friends, which made me think of Scribblehopper.

Poor friend, I needed to find him and save him! Who knows where Nebula, Wither's evil ally, had IMPRISONED him.

I thought about my frog friend as we scaled the volcano once more. We had to toss that gem inside. It was a matter of life and death!

When at last we reached the top of the volcano, I stared down into the crater at the bubbling **MOLTEN LAVA**.

"Quickly, Defender, throw the **CRYSTAL GEM**!" my friends urged.

With trembling paws I took the sack with the gem from

around my neck. Then I pulled out the gem and threw it in. Suddenly, however, a gray CLOUD quickly materialized into a shape that I knew well . . .

It was NEBULA! She reached out her hand to grab the gem, crying out triumphantly, "I knew I would win in the end, you furry rat fool!"

Don't even think about stopping us!

She was about to grab the gem when . . .

Mosquitina leaped quickly to the attack and stung Nebula's hand.

"Yowchie!" cried Nebula, forgetting for a moment about the gem.

And that was all it took. The Crystal Gem fell down, down, down, and a moment later, the bright red lava swallowed it up.

Right at that moment, the volcano exploded in a

FLASH OF BLUE LIGHT!

We closed our eyes and hid our faces from that blinding light, then the ground beneath us began to shake and shake and shake . . .

A wonderful scent spread all around us and when we opened our eyes we realized that

something

EXTRAORDINARY

had happened!

THE PEACE PEAK

We did it! Nebula was defeated! Thanks to the Crystal Gem, the great FIERY ABYSS had turned into a fabumouse Crystal mountain where everything was peaceful!

From the top of the mountain there appeared a beautiful . . .

rainbow.

That's what always happens in the Kingdom of Fantasy when great danger has been avoided! Beautiful arcs of color come out of the sky.

Solo exclaimed solemnly, "This mountain from now on will be called the Peace Peak."

I smiled. Thanks to all of my AMAZING friends, we had managed to bring peace to the Kingdom of Fantasy.

YAY FOR US! LONG LIVE BLOSSOM! SCORE ONE FOR THE GEM TEAM! LONG LIVE PEACE!

I thanked each of my friends and hugged them all one by one. They really were the best. Still, I couldn't help but be worried. My mission wasn't truly finished yet. Yes, we had defeated the **Darkshadow** and brought peace to the Kingdom of Fantasy. But I hadn't found Blossom's precious child, Winglet. Where could she be? I had to bring her home!

"What's wrong?" Wolfy asked me, watching as I began **TWISTING** my tail up in knots. **OUCH!**

"I still need to finish my mission and find Winglet," I explained. I promised Queen Blossom. "And the worst part is I don't even know where to look. Not even Mel the Magnificent could find her in his magic **Ball of Marvels**!"

"It's okay." The **VON WILD** brothers comforted me, patting my shoulder. "We'll go with you to search for her. We'll all meet at **CRYSTAL CASTLE**, all of us, Mosquitina, Solo . . . the whole Gem Team! We'll put our heads together and come up with a plan. Together, we can find her and bring her back."

Bluewing flew around my head, shouting, "Guardian, you can count on the **mini-dragon clan** as well! With this **whistle** I'll call everyone together and we can help with the search."

Reassured by my friends' support, I began to feel like maybe all was not lost.

"Let's go!" I squeaked. But then I realized it would take me **forever** to walk all the

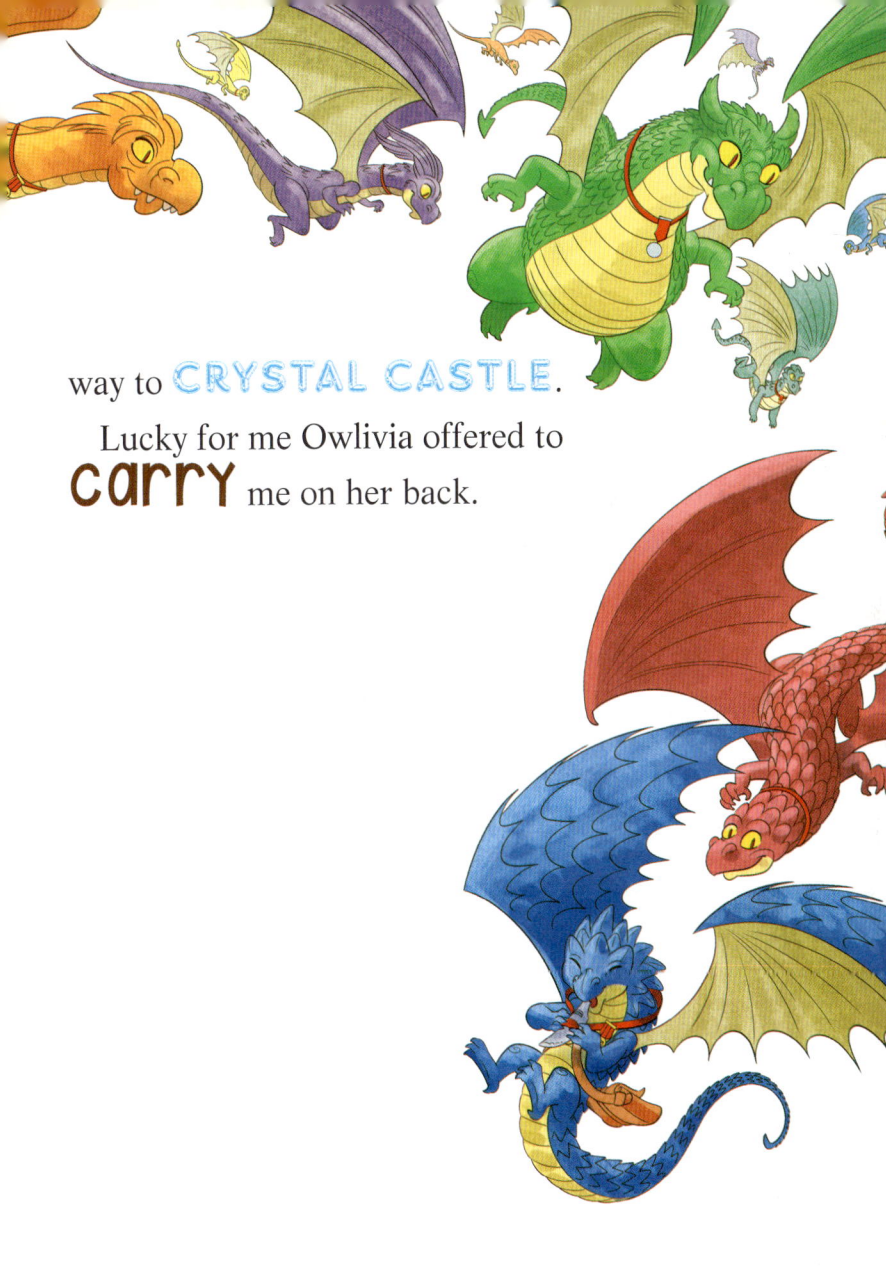

way to CRYSTAL CASTLE.

Lucky for me Owlivia offered to carry me on her back.

THE MOST BEAUTIFUL CASTLE!

When I reached Crystal Castle, I found Queen Blossom on the balcony of her room, along with her husband, George. They stood staring off into the distance at the Bright Mountains. They looked so sad. I felt awful.

"I'm very sorry I let you down," I told the queen. "I haven't been able to find little Winglet."

She sighed. "It's okay, Bright Defender. I know you did your best, which is all we can ask of ourselves. I have full faith in you and if you couldn't find our daughter, then we will just have to accept she is gone forever."

Tears rolled down Blossom's sweet face. Oh, what a terrible tragedy!

It was killing me knowing that the queen was

heartbroken. So I promised her that I wouldn't leave the Kingdom of Fantasy until I found little Winglet. As soon as I said it, I began to feel **HOMESICK**. Maybe I could get my friends back in *New Mouse City* to send a care package.

Guardian!

My Queen!

To cheer Blossom up I told her about having defeated the Darkshadow. She congratulated me on my success, along with CLEVER CHAMELEON, who had just arrived.

"The time has come to return Crystal Castle to the Kingdom of Fairies!" he declared. Then he added to me under his breath, "Let's hope that this helps Queen Blossom get her sweet smile back."

Suddenly, she began to sing softly.

My castle, it's time to depart,
And go back to the Kingdom's heart.
Travel fast, faster than light,
Travel far with all of your might!
Get to my kingdom safe and sound,
and soon my baby shall be found!
A mother's heart knows what shall be,
As sure as waves crash in the sea!

At that moment, the castle lifted into the air and began to fly. I was so surprised we were moving, I completely forgot to hang on to something. I fell over with a **clunk**!

oooofff!

My glasses broke into a thousand pieces.

PLiNK!

Uh-oh. Without **glasses** I can't see one whisker!

Then I remembered that Mel had given me a pair of

ENCHANTED GLASSES.

I took them from inside my armor and **slipped** them on. I looked around anxiously. Phew! They worked!

I was able to see really well. Those glasses were truly **magical**!

Heeeeelp!

As the castle *zoomed* along through the sky (Oh, why did the queen tell it to move so fast? Did I mention I'm afraid to fly?) I STUMBLED back onto my feet.

Eventually I managed to LEAN against the wall and make my way down the long, long hallway.

That's when I found myself in front of Winglet's room.

THE MOST  BEAUTIFUL CASTLE!

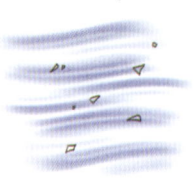

BADABAMMM!

J ust as I passed the door of Winglet's room, a strong gust of wind made the door burst open . . .

IT WAS THE WESTERN WIND!

BADABAMMM!!!

BADABAAAMM!

With sadness I gazed inside the room, thinking of that basinet that was empty and might remain that way forever.

I noticed that the Western Wind kept BLOWING around the silk curtains. It was almost like it was trying to get my attention. HOW strange!

Slowly, I made my way into the room and peeked into the **crib**. **Holy Swiss rolls on rye!** I couldn't believe my eyes! A child was **sleeping** inside it!

I took off my enchanted glasses and looked again. Now it was empty!

Then I understood. Thanks to the **magic glasses** I was able to see baby Winglet. She had been there all along but she was **invisible**

I can't believe my eyes!

because she was the victim of an evil spell!

Winglet was never far from home. Actually she was there, in her room, close to those who loved her.

I cleaned my glasses and looked once more into the crib. The most beautiful **BABY** I had ever seen was sleeping with her head on a silk pillow.

Her hair was **blue** like the spring sky, and her skin was clear like the **moonlight** and had a delicate light blue hue to it like all of the **Winged Ones**. She had **long**, feathery eyelashes and the *sweetest* smile.

I tried to call her by whispering, "Baby Winglet! Can you hear me? I'm the Bright Guardian. Time to wake up."

But the eyes of the child remained closed.

I took her in my arms and tried again, "Wake up, *princess*!"

But she *slept and slept and slept . . .*

and slept . . . and slept . . .
and slept . . . and slept . . .
and slept . . . and slept . . .
and slept . . . and slept . . .

and slep
and slep
and slept

WINGLET'S REAWAKENING

A REAL LOVE SPELL

Holding **WiNglet** in my arms, I yelled with all my might, "Queen Blossom! I found her!" My voice echoed in the **EMPTY** corridors of the Crystal Castle, **bouncing** off the crystalline walls.

I found the little Princess!

My baby?

Immediately, Blossom and her husband came **running**, followed by her **advisors** and the fairy court. Mosquitina and the Von Wild Brothers, Wolfy and her *friends*, and all the mini-dragons were there, too. They gathered around me with puzzled expressions.

Blossom ran to me with her arms open. "You found my baby? Where is she? I don't see her!"

Winglet?!

Really?!

Finally!

I held the baby out to her. "She is here in my arms!" I explained.

But Blossom shook her head. "I don't see anything," she sighed.

Only then did I remember the enchanted glasses. Quickly, I took them off and passed them to Blossom.

As soon as the queen put those magic glasses on, her face lit up with joy. "It's her, it's really her, my little Winglet!" she cried happily. She held her tight in her arms and rockeD her, but the baby didn't wake up.

Blossom turned to me, worried. "Why isn't she waking up?

I told the queen my theory. The princess was under some kind of evil sleeping spell. Besides sleeping, the spell also made her invisible, which is why no one could find her.

Blossom's husband hugged her as the queen

stared sadly at little Winglet **sleeping** soundly in her arms.

I was thrilled we had found Winglet. If only she wasn't in a **bewitched sleep**!

Just then the fairy godmother stepped forward and looked kindly at Blossom. "I know how to wake the little one, Your Majesty," she said. "We need a very **powerful** spell to balance out all the evil of this witchcraft. We need . . .

a real l♥ve spell!"

My little one!

LOVE BEATS EVIL

Blossom gently put the little one into the *bassinet*, grabbed her magic wand, and spun around three times, singing,

*"Love beats evil
Every time.
Curse be gone.
Now let love shine!"*

But the baby remained invisible, so she tried again,

*"Love beats evil
Every time.
Curse be gone,
Now let love shine!"*

Still nothing happened. I could tell Blossom was really disappointed, but then a glimmer of hope appeared in her eyes.

"This SPELL is too powerful," she said. "I can't destroy it alone. But there is a SOLUTION. If you help me, your hearts together with mine can destroy it."

So we all joined hands and sang,

"Love beats evil
Every time.
Curse be gone,
Now let love shine!"

Suddenly, there was a *flash of light* and the baby was visible once more!

Everyone crowded around the crib and cried out,

"Ooooh, there's little Winglet! She's so beautiful!"

I was thrilled the baby was now visible, but she was still sleeping. Did we need another spell?

Before I could ask, Blossom stepped toward the crib. "All she needs now is a true love's kiss," she said softly, bending down to give the baby a kiss on her forehead.

At that moment, the child woke up. She opened her eyes, which were as blue as cornflowers, and smiled a smile as sweet as the smell of flowers in spring!

"Welcome back, darling!" Blossom said, lifting the baby into her arms.

Now that I had found Winglet there was only one more **mystery** left to solve. Where, oh, where was my dear frog friend, **SCRIBBLEHOPPER**?

Right then my eyes fell on the strange **STATUE** of Scribblehopper that I had seen before in little Winglet's room.

UMM, HOW STRANGE!

I patted the statue with my paw. It looked just like my frog friend, except with a **BLUISH TINT**. In fact, the statue was made of **PURE** crystal.

I wondered who had made a statue of Scribblehopper and why the expression on his face look so **terrified**.

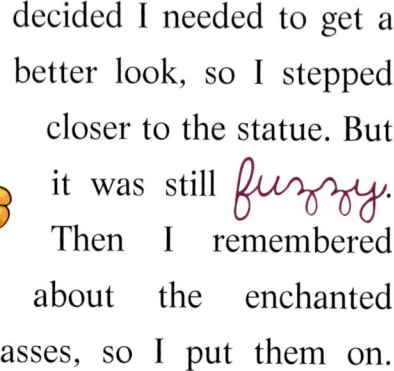

I decided I needed to get a better look, so I stepped closer to the statue. But it was still *fuzzy*. Then I remembered about the enchanted glasses, so I put them on. That's when I understood! The **enchanted glasses** let me see that it wasn't actually a crystal statue, it was **SCRIBBLEHOPPER**, and he had been **crystallized** by an evil spell!

"Help!" I called to Blossom. "Scribblehopper is **trapped** in that crystal statue!"

She quickly got her wand and ordered,

"Release this frog! Let him hop and be free.
Release him from this wicked spell,
for all the world to see!"

As soon as Blossom uttered those words, the

statue lit up and began to *VIBRATE* ...

It *VIBRATED* more and more until it broke apart. In the end, from that pile of crystal dust, my frog friend popped up.

Everyone yelled, "Scribblehopper has returned!"

"Well, actually I've been here the whole time. I tried to tell you but no one seemed to hear me or you were all just ignoring me! Humph!"

Oh, how I missed my old friend!

WINGS ENCHANTED, WINGS OF LIGHT!

Blossom was **glowing** with happiness. No, seriously, she was actually **glowing**. Though maybe it had something to do with her **bluish tint** or the fact that she was standing near a light. She announced, "I would like to celebrate someone here today. Someone very **special**."

I looked around. Was it someone's birthday? Anniversary? Graduation from Fairy School?

I want to honor you!

Then I realized that the queen and everyone else were staring at me. Instantly my fur turned **beet red**. Yes, it turns out, I, Geronimo Stilton, was the someone special! I was so surprised thinking about my special new status that I forgot to listen to half of what the queen was saying. **OOPS.**

When I tuned in a moment later I heard her saying something about giving me a special gift that no one but those in the *Winged Dynasty* possess.

"It is a power that that will make you stronger so that you can defend the Kingdom of Fantasy," she was saying.

Then she added that I would be part of the family and I should also call her "sister."

Everyone in the court shouted,

"Oooooh, What an honor!"

THE POWER OF THE WINGED ONES

The Winged Dynasty has always reigned over the Kingdom of Fantasy. They have light blue skin, transparent wings, and pure hearts.

BLOSSOM is the flower queen, the lady of peace, she who carries the harmony of the world . . . and she is also the queen of the fairies!

Her father is Tick Tock, the wizard of time; Sproutness, the fairy of the earth, is her sister, and Solitaire is her brother. George, the king of dreams, is Blossom's husband.

Each one has special powers. Tick Tock, for example, regulates the passing of time in the Kingdom of Fantasy; Sproutness makes seeds grow with her songs; and Blossom can read the hearts of every creature in the Kingdom. But one of the secret powers that all Winged Ones have is that they can transform into dragonings, which are also known as the Dragons of Light! They are strong, luminous, and pure. The dragonings defend peace and harmony from the evil plots of the Darkest in the Kingdom of Fantasy. Now the Bright Guardian will also be a dragoning and will be able to always defend the Kingdom of Fantasy.

I was thinking that it seemed a little **odd** to call Blossom my sister (after all, I already have a sister at home in New Mouse City). But I didn't want to offend the queen, so I just smiled. What could I say?

And even though the whole sister thing seemed rather strange, a minute later the queen gave me the **coolest** gift. Apparently, she was giving me the **power** to transform myself into a **dragoning**! What is a **dragoning**? It is a dragon of **LIGHT**! And Blossom said I would be the strongest one of all!

Next the queen spun around three times and said,

"Wings of light
Come to me.
Reward this mouse
For bravery.
Give him strength,
And with these wings,
He will be a dragoning!"

ONE MOMENT, JUST ONE MOMENT . . .

As everyone congratulated me, Moonflower, the nurse, who had just **arrived**, stepped forward. "Oh, finally little Winglet has been found! I'm so happy! What a relief!"

She approached Blossom, extending her arms, "Oh, My Queen, let me hold her once more in my arms!"

My little treasure . . .

But Blossom headed toward the crib. "I would prefer to put her back in her crib and bring it to my room. From now on Winglet will always stay close to me. After everything that happened, I don't want her out of my sight for a single moment," she said.

The nurse looked offended. "I just want to hold her for a moment," she insisted.

Blossom, however, had already put the baby in the basinet. "Don't be offended, dear *Moonflower*, but as I said, from now on I will be the only one to care for her," she explained.

For some reason the nurse refused to take no for an answer. She neared the crib muttering, "Let me hold her . . ."

Only then did I realize I wasn't wearing the enchanted glasses.

Hastily, I put them on and suddenly before me I saw the most horrifying sight. The nurse fairy

transformed into a witch. It was **WITHER**, Blossom's evil sister!

I yelled, "Your Majesty, watch out! She's not a fairy, she's a witch! It's Wither!

But it was *too late*! Wither had already grabbed the baby and was holding her close with a crazed look in her eyes.

Oh, what a sweet nurse!

"Don't even think of stopping me! I will bring the child with me and raise her to be far more wicked than yours truly. But don't fear, I will soon return to reign over the entire Kingdom of Fantasy!" she cackled.

Right then an enormouse crow flew into the open window!

But that's Wither!

He had feathers as black as ink and a **copper** beak. I recognized him at once,

CROWBAR THE CRUEL,

Wither's evil husband!

He cawed,

"Oh, my wife, My Dark Majesty,

Our Dark Kingdom awaits.

Come home now with me!"

Wither yelled and ran toward him, **clutching** little Winglet, who was wailing loudly.

I was feeling *hopeless* when suddenly

I remembered about my new power. I could transform into a dragon! If I could only remember the words Blossom told me to recite in order to become a **dragoning**. Something about light and power and dragons . . .

At last they came to me and I shouted, "Power of light, power of wings, turn me into a dragoning!"

I felt an enormouse power as two huge **dragon wings** shot out of my back! My paws grew long claws and my huge **DRAGON** tail was covered in pointy scales.

Even though I felt energized, a sense of calm came over me. Who knew being a dragon could be so relaxing?

GIVE ME THE BABY!

I opened my mouth to **yeLL** at Wither, and my voice came out in a powerful dragon roar. Whoa! I almost scared myself! "Give me that baby at once!" I roared.

Rrrroaaaarrrrrr!

Not surprisingly, Crowbar the Cruel laughed in my face, and Wither **WAVED** her wand in the air. "Good luck finding us in the dark!" she cackled.

Rats! The witch had turned **day** into **NIGHT**! I would have to fight them in the **INKY** darkness!

I was struggling to adjust to the **DARK**

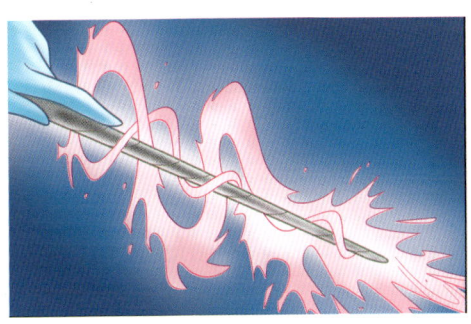

when I felt Crowbar the Cruel attacking me with his **SHARP** copper beak. At the same time, Wither began **stabbing** me in the side with her **pointy** wand. Luckily, I was wearing the **armor of light** that Clever Chameleon had given me.

I was feeling pretty invincible when Crowbar came at me with his talons. **OUCH!**

I wasn't expecting the sudden attack, and I was caught by surprise.

His **claws** managed to miss my armor and instead cut a DELICATE membrane in my wings. Drops of my dragon blood fell to the ground.

Oh, how I hate the sight of blood!

Still, when I heard the baby CRY I felt a surge of energy.

Crowbar and Wither could not handle the *purity* of that light.

Crowbar swerved and lost control, cawing, "**Noooooooo!**"

Wither covered her face with her hands, shouting, "NOOOOOOOOO!"

In that moment, disturbed by the purity of the light, **WITHER** thought only of hiding herself. She forgot that she had the baby in her arms and let the baby fall. Luckily, I was ready and darted down to **GRAB** her in the air!

The crowd all yelled, "**Oooooh!**"

A superpowerful and pure light shot out of the Sword of Light!

You'll Never Win!

The two **wicked** ones flew away defeated. "We'll be back! And next time we will win!" they called over their shoulders.

This got the mini-dragons' blood boiling. "You'll never be winners!" they shrieked. "You'll never win against the **BRIGHT GUARDIAN**, or Queen Blossom. Good always conquers bad in the end. We will always be here to help protect Princess Winglet!"

I was just relieved it was finally over and Winglet was safe.

The mini-dragons all gathered

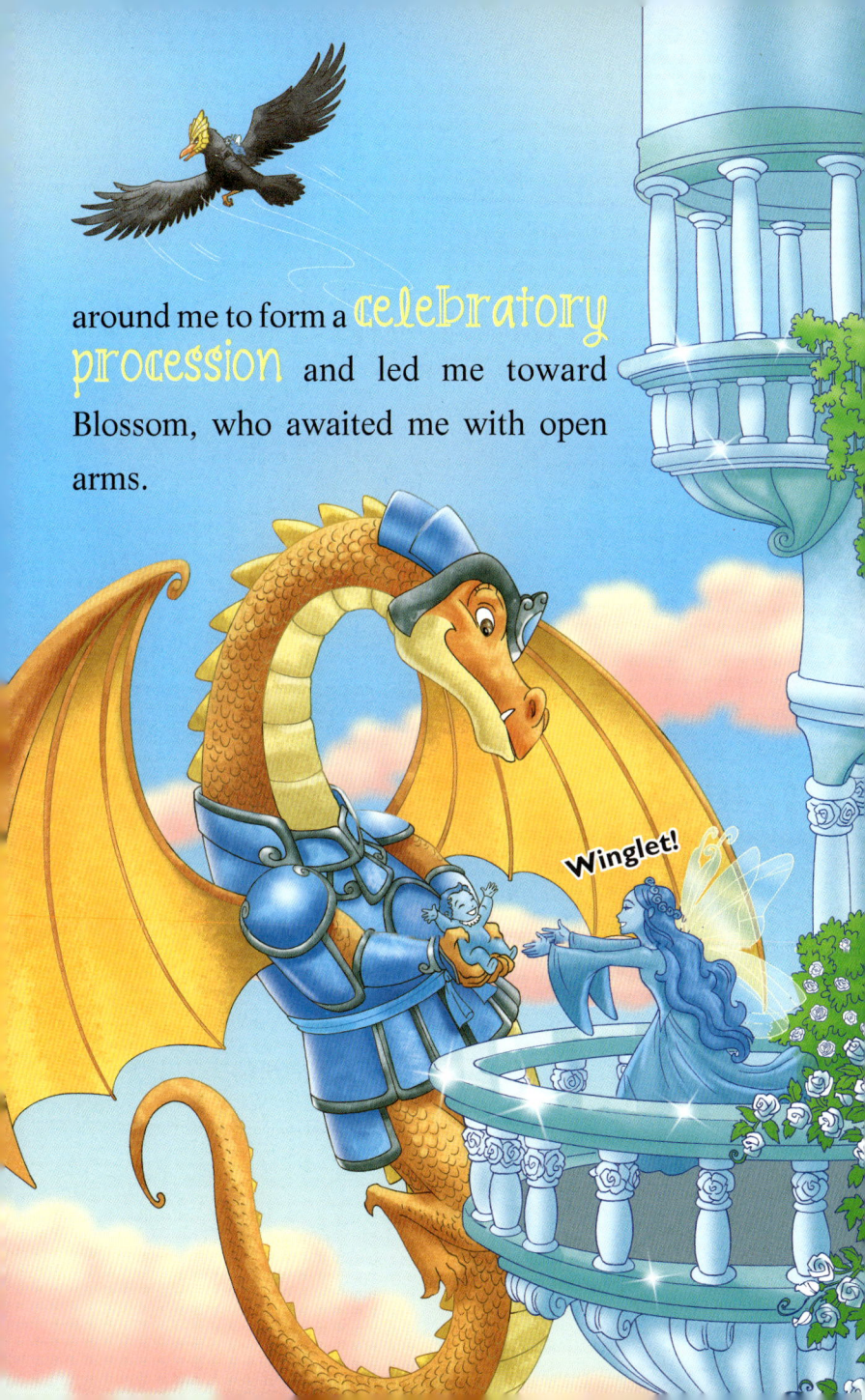

around me to form a celebratory procession and led me toward Blossom, who awaited me with open arms.

Winglet!

I put her baby in her arms and we all **BREATHED** a sigh of relief. At last baby Winglet was back where she belonged!

I looked around and saw that we had returned to the **Kingdom OF Fairies.**

Hurray for the Spiny Grub!

As soon as Crystal Castle was back on its foundation, Blossom spoke with the Ceremony Fairy who began to write something down. I had no idea what the fairy was writing, and I was too **tired** to care. The queen led me to a guest room so I could rest. There, I found a new pair of **glasses** on the nightstand, but I didn't put them on. Instead, I threw myself onto the bed and instantly fell into a **DEEP** sleep. I slept and slept and slept . . .

SLEPT AND SLEPT

I woke up **hours** and **hours** later when a fairy rudely smacked me on the snout. Well, okay, first she knocked on my door, but I guess I didn't wake up, so she yelled in my ear and I still didn't wake up, so she SMACKED me on the snout. Can I help it if I'm not a morning mouse?

Anyway, where was I? Ah yes, the fairy led me to the queen, who brought me onto a balcony.

"Dear brother, I have a surprise for you," she announced.

Beneath the balcony there was an enormouse crowd filled with all the inhabitants of the Kingdom of Fantasy. They cheered,

"LONG LIVE THE DRAGONING!"

"Hurray for the Bright Defender!"

I noticed that the **GEM TEAM** that had come back to Crystal Castle was in the crowd, too, and there was a small orchestra playing beautiful music. The mini-dragons were there, too, waving flags and streamers and yelling, "Long live the dragoning! You're our heroooo!"

FlΔP! FlΔP! FlΔP!

Then a group of mini-dragons lifted off in flight and reached the balcony carrying an enormouse **SPiNY GRUB CAKE**!

The mini-dragons held out the enormouse cake as they whispered back and forth to one another.

"You tell him!"

"No you tell him!"

"But I'm shy!"

"I am, too!"

"Oh, all right, we will all tell him together . . .

"This special cake is just for you.

It's not a medal that is true,

It's filled with thanks for all you've done.

And spiny grub herbs by the ton.

Please eat it up, now don't be shy.

It's better than mom's apple pie."

Flap! Flap! Flap!

I turned pale. How would I ever be able to eat a cake made of stinky spiny grub?!

Right then BLUEWING arrived. He was carrying a GIANT pill given to dragons when they have an upset stomach. All I had to do was eat the pill and my stomach would be fine, he explained. There was only one problem. The pill was **ENORMOUSE**!

I was starting to **panic** when I noticed *Blossom* chuckling. She leaned over and, winking, told me, "Don't worry about eating the cake. Remember you can transform into a **dragoning**. Dragonings love spiny grub!"

Hee, hee, hee!

Take Me with You!

Now that my mission was completed, it was time for me to return home to **MOUSE ISLAND**.

I said good-bye to Blossom, who at that moment was having a meeting

Argh!

Flap! Flap!

with her people in the CEREMONY ROOM. As soon as she saw me, she ordered, "Bring another **CRYSTAL THRONE** for my dear brother! I want him to sit next to me!"

I sat on the **shiny** crystal throne, which was lined with a **soft blue cushion**. On the throne in small letters was etched the word **dragoning**.

Here's the throne!

It's for the Defender!

The Gem Team and all the friends I had made during that adventure lined up to say good-bye and wish me a safe trip.

Even Mel arrived to congratulate me. "Who would've have guessed you could do it? Not me!"

BLUEWING was the most emotional. He sobbed, "No, don't go! I will miss you too much." Then he added, "Hey, I have an idea. Take me with you!"

I tried to patiently explain that I had my family, my friends, and my work waiting for me at home. And more important, that a

really belonged in the Kingdom of Fantasy. But he didn't seem to get what I was saying.

He grabbed my sleeve with his little claws

and wouldn't let go. "You've just got to take me with you," he begged. "You'll see, I won't bother you, I'm small, I wouldn't get in the way, you won't even know I'm around."

Yep, that mini-dragon was just like a STARVING mouse with a fresh block of CHEESE. He wasn't giving it up without a fight!

More than anything BLUEWING insisted he loved to travel. "I love going on adventures and I think I would love visiting Mouse Island," he said. "I never tasted CHEESE — it must be delicious. And if you want, I can dress up like a mouse. What would it take, a pair of fake ears and a tail? I could be the perfect mouse!"

The mini-dragon yammered

I can't bring you!

Pleeeeaaase!

on and on and on until I could hardly think straight. Then out of the corner of my eye I spotted Owlivia.

"Do you think you could take me back to the **real world**, to my home on Mouse Island soon? It's been great here in the Kingdom of Fantasy but I miss my *family* and my **friends**," I squeaked.

Owlivia smiled. "You don't need me to go back," she said.

Huh? What did she mean? A minute later I remembered. I was a **dragoning**! That meant I could go and come back whenever I wanted to! All I had to do was TRANSFORM myself!

"Before you leave for good, though, I have to ask you to check the borders between the real world and the Kingdom of Fantasy," Blossom said. "Since you'll always be our BRIGHT DEFENDER."

I **chewed** my whiskers. Don't get me wrong, I love helping out the queen and I know defending the Kingdom of Fantasy from evildoers is important. But it is, and probably always will be, a very, very, very **DANGEROUS** job, and though I've come a long way, I, Geronimo Stilton, am still a *'fraidy mouse* at heart. (Shhh! Don't tell anyone!)

I said good-bye to everyone, and everyone said

You don't need me to go back!

Huh?

good-bye to me. Scribblehopper wrapped me in a **bone-crunching** hug (**squeak!**). He thanked me again and again for saving him. Then he whipped out a huge basket filled with tons of **frog** food for the trip back.

Inside the basket I found gnat candies, a fly tart, a **maggot smoothie**, and a jar full of swamp mud to put on **water-lily bread**.

I thanked him, and then I looked for **BLUEWING**, but I couldn't find him!

Who knows where my **little** mini-dragon friend had ended up?

Then I announced, "Umm, so, then, I guess I'll be off . . ."

I scratched my head. For the life of me, I couldn't remember what to say to transform myself into a **dragoning**. Fortunately, Owlivia came to my rescue. She whispered the chant in my ear.

Then I cleared my throat and repeated it:

Power of light, power of wings, turn me into a dragoning!

HOME SWEET HOME

I flew and flew all night long, heading toward the borders of the Kingdom of Fantasy. I made sure that there were no open **gaps** that any witches could use to pass through. Everything was in place, and the **borders** between the Kingdom of Fantasy and the real world were protected.

I breathed a sigh of **RELIEF**. Thank goodmouse, my **duty** as the Bright Defender was done.

Reassured, I headed toward the great vortex of light that marked the border between this Kingdom and the real world. I couldn't wait to get home on my beloved Mouse Island! to my sweet mouse home!

And that's how I crossed through the **VORTEX OF LIGHT** that took me back to my very own New Mouse City. When I arrived on the balcony of my house I had been changed into a mouse again. *Squeak!* It was night and, as always happens when I travel in the Kingdom of Fantasy, it was the exact time that I had left. That's right, time had stopped! The only thing **different** about me was that I was still dressed in my suit of armor. Oops!

I'm in New Mouse City!

FLAP! FLAP! FLAP!

Later that night, I poured myself a nice, piping-hot cup of **hot chocolate** and cut myself a decent-sized chunk of Parmesan. It looked so good I'm embarrassed to say I was practically drooling!

I sat down at the kitchen table and as I was about to eat the first mouthful, I heard a little voice shriek, "Yum, that must be good cheese!"

"Who said that?!" I squeaked.

Then I heard a familiar sound. Flap! Flap! Flap!

Suddenly, a **blue** head popped out from behind a piece of furniture. "Cheeeese! I haven't tasted it but it smells delicious!" a voice said.

It was BLUEWING!

"Wh-wh-what are you doing here?" I stammered.

The mini-dragon didn't seem to hear me. He seemed mesmerized by my cheese. A second later, he **flung** himself onto the hunk of Parmesan and began chewing.

GNAM GNAMM GNAMMM!

"Whoa!" he shrieked. "This stuff is better than **spiny grub**!"

Next thing I knew, Bluewing jumped onto the table and began singing,

Gnammm!

"There's no mistaking it,
Cheese is a major hit.
Spiny grub I used to love,
But cheese might be a step above!"

Then he began jumping all over at warp speed. He flew onto the refrigerator, and then he crashed into a stack of pots. **Crash!** What a mess!

Before I could yell "Stop!" he threw open the fridge door and jumped in, sampling everything he could get his **claws** on. "What is this? **YOGURT?** We don't have that in the Kingdom of Fantasy! And what's this? **Ice cream?**

Clang!

Good! Yum! This 'constantly cold closet' is the best!"

Then he saw some **lollipops** and grabbed a handful, shrieking, "I can give these to my friends back home!"

I ran after him, trying to stop him, but he

For my friends!

was unstoppable! He ran into the living room, and with dirty, chocolate-covered claws, he jumped on my couch and turned on the television with the volume all the way up, yelling, "What is this box, with all these magical pictures that move and talk? A t-e-l-e-v-i-s-i-o-n?

"I love it! And these cartoons are greeeaaaat!"

Then he ran into my bathroom and took a shower, getting suds all over my floor as he sang at the top of his lungs,

What's this?

"I love it here
This place is great!
Don't make me go,
I'll be up at eight!"

With that he slipped into the drawer of my nightstand, wrapped himself up in my scarf, and fell fast asleep . . .

SNORE... SNORE... SNORE...

I stared down at the mini-dragon snoring peacefully with a smile on his face. Even though he could drive a mouse crazy, I must confess it was hard not to smile back.

What a Day!

The next morning I went to the office. I didn't want to leave BLUEWING alone, so I stuck him in my pocket, wrapped in my scarf so he could stay warm.

As I walked down the street I said hi to all my friends. The sky was blue and CLEAR, and the sun was *shining* brightly.

Bluewing, who was super-curious, stuck his head out of the edge of my pocket, asking thousands of questions: "What is t-a-x-i? And that? A b-i-c-y-c-l-e? Wow, I would like to have a little bicycle. Could you find one suitable for a mini-dragon? And what's that store over there with that delicious smell coming from it? A b-a-k-e-r-y? Can we go there? I want to taste a c-r-o-i-s-s-a-n-t!"

These sweets are tasty!

When we reached the office, he **jUMpeD** into the drawer of my desk, where I kept all my **snacks**, and had some. Then he took **a nap** wrapped in

Snore!

my scarf. Finally, he **jumped** on the keyboard of my computer, yelling, "Can I send an **email** to my mini-dragon friends? How do I write?"

Then he grabbed my **phone** and began calling all my friends.

I want to send an email!

"I am Geronimo Stilton's new

It's Bluewing!

assistant. My name is Bluewing and who are you? You're nice!" he yelled.

To surprise him, I bought him a little bicycle at a toy store. He circled around the room, shrieking, "Whee! Look at me go!"

Hee, hee, hee!

I Miss Spiny Grub!

Days passed, and Bluewing was happy staying with me. He seemed to enjoy living in the **mouse world**, which was so different from his own. He said it was a great dragon adventure.

But after a few weeks, I noticed that the mini-dragon seemed sad. One night, he jumped around my neck and **hugged** me. **Tears** sprang to his eyes.

"What's wrong?" I asked, concerned.

Soon the mini-dragon was **SOBBING** up a storm. He explained how much he loved living in my **house** and trying new things and meeting all of my mouse

Waaaah!

friends. But he missed his home in the Kingdom of Fantasy and the other mini-dragons. "Plus, I know I said I loved cheese, but now I'm missing the spiny grub! I want to go home! Can you take me back to the Kingdom of Fantasy?" he asked.

And so, at dawn, when the first rays of sun lit up the Mouse City sky, I put on my armor once more. Then I took Bluewing in my arms, went to the balcony of my house, and yelled,

"Power of light, power of wings, turn me into a dragoning!"

Immediately, a flash of light surrounded me, and a moment later, my body transformed into an enormouse, powerful, superstrong dragon . . .

And that's how my next trip to the

KINGDOM OF FANTASY

started.

But that is another story for another time.

A story of **FANTASY**, adventure, and, of course, **friendship**.

I give you my word, Geronimo Stilton's word!

FANTASIAN ALPHABET

ABOUT THE AUTHOR

 Born in New Mouse City, Mouse Island, **GERONIMO STILTON** is Rattus Emeritus of Mousomorphic Literature and of Neo-Ratonic Comparative Philosophy. For the past twenty years, he has been running *The Rodent's Gazette*, New Mouse City's most widely read daily newspaper.

Stilton was awarded the Ratitzer Prize for his scoops on *The Curse of the Cheese Pyramid* and *The Search for Sunken Treasure*. He has also received the Andersen 2000 Prize for Personality of the Year. One of his bestsellers won the 2002 eBook Award for world's best ratlings' electronic book. His works have been published all over the globe.

In his spare time, Mr. Stilton collects antique cheese rinds and plays golf. But what he most enjoys is telling stories to his nephew Benjamin.

Don't miss any of my adventures in the Kingdom of Fantasy!

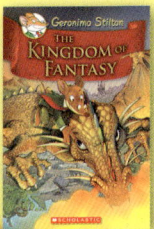

THE KINGDOM OF FANTASY

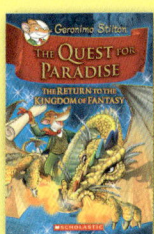

THE QUEST FOR PARADISE: THE RETURN TO THE KINGDOM OF FANTASY

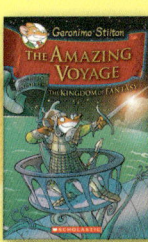

THE AMAZING VOYAGE: THE THIRD ADVENTURE IN THE KINGDOM OF FANTASY

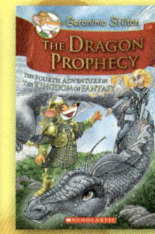

THE DRAGON PROPHECY: THE FOURTH ADVENTURE IN THE KINGDOM OF FANTASY

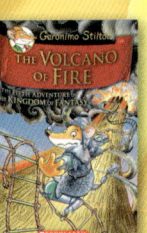

THE VOLCANO OF FIRE: THE FIFTH ADVENTURE IN THE KINGDOM OF FANTASY

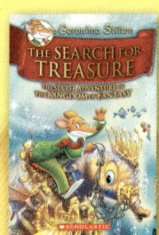

THE SEARCH FOR TREASURE: THE SIXTH ADVENTURE IN THE KINGDOM OF FANTASY

THE ENCHANTED CHARMS: THE SEVENTH ADVENTURE IN THE KINGDOM OF FANTASY

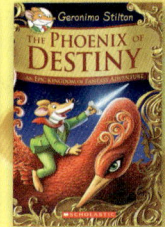

THE PHOENIX OF DESTINY: AN EPIC KINGDOM OF FANTASY ADVENTURE

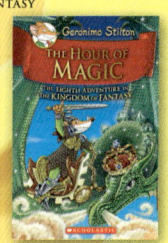

THE HOUR OF MAGIC: THE EIGHTH ADVENTURE IN THE KINGDOM OF FANTASY

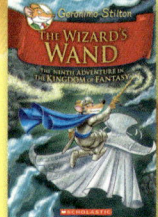

THE WIZARD'S WAND: THE NINTH ADVENTURE IN THE KINGDOM OF FANTASY

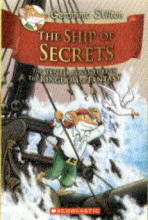

THE SHIP OF SECRETS: THE TENTH ADVENTURE IN THE KINGDOM OF FANTASY

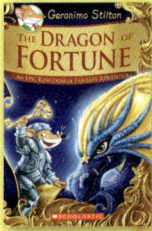

THE DRAGON OF FORTUNE: AN EPIC KINGDOM OF FANTASY ADVENTURE

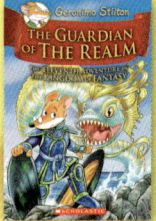

THE GUARDIAN OF THE REALM: THE ELEVENTH ADVENTURE IN THE KINGDOM OF FANTASY

Join me and my friends as we hunt for answers in these special edition mysteries!

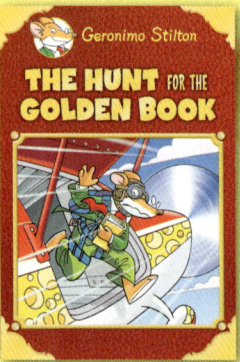

The Hunt for the Golden Book

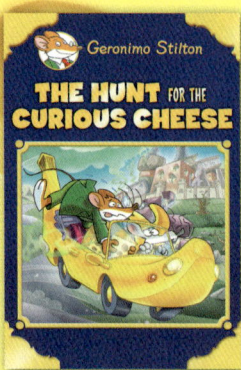

The Hunt for the Curious Cheese

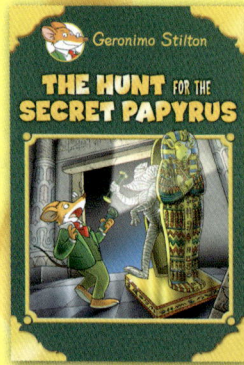

The Hunt for the Secret Papyrus

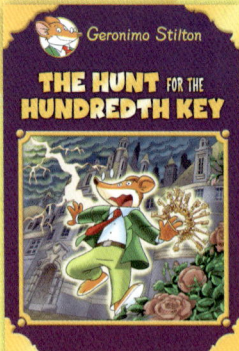

The Hunt for the Hundredth Key

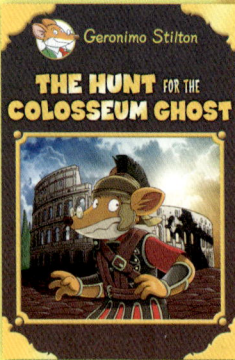

The Hunt for the Colosseum Ghost